# A SOLDIER

# KNOWN

# UNTO GOD

W. J. Featherstone

# Dedication

This book is dedicated to the fond memory of my grandparents who, like countless others of their generation, so willingly served their country during the bloodiest conflict the world had ever seen.

# Acknowledgements

My heartfelt thanks to Olivia, Chad, Stefan, Susie, Mary, Dilly and Richard for their encouragement, enthusiasm, literary and technical help, without which this book would not have been published.

W. J. F.

# Disclaimer

The following story is just that: a story, a work of fiction. Whilst historical personages and events, institutions, organisations and businesses mentioned are factual and many of the locations referred to are real places, they are used purely in a fictitious manner.

The village of Bucksleigh is a product of the author's imagination, as are the characters in the story. Any resemblance to actual people, living or dead, is completely coincidental.

W. J. Featherstone

August 2019

# CONTENTS

# REFLECTION

During the night it had snowed - not heavily, but enough to demonstrate that winter had not yet relinquished its grip upon the landscape. A pale, feeble sun staggered drunkenly into the chill morning sky, its cold light chasing away the remnants of the stars that had stood like sentinels over the sleeping countryside during the dark hours and which now lingered obstinately into the grey dawn. Far below, the folds of hills and rolling meadows and the silhouettes of spartan trees laced with snow, emerged gradually out of the gloom, to take on shape and substance for another day.

Outside the tiny, slate-roofed cottage nothing stirred, except for the thin wisps of smoke which curled intermittently into the morning air from the squat, brick chimney, the final throes of life from the smouldering embers in the hearth below; all that now remained from the roaring fire of farewell the previous evening.

The memory of that final evening lingered still, as his mind scrambled its way from the soothing abyss of slumber and into full consciousness. For some moments he lay motionless, exulting in the soporific comfort of the broad, soft featherbed and wallowed gratefully in the quiet of the early morning stillness. The only sound was the gentle rhythm of Amy breathing, as she lay next to him, still sleeping soundly.

Presently, he slipped noiselessly from beneath the sheets and, padding softly to the tiny window, drew back the heavy, brown woollen curtains to gaze out onto the frosted fields and hedgerows. He breathed in deeply, as if trying to absorb something of the tranquillity and gentleness of his surroundings, as if that in itself might help to banish the horror and nightmare of the past two years.

Almost fearfully, he turned slowly and studied himself in the large, oak-framed mirror glowering from the cream-painted wall of the tiny bedroom. He looked a mere ghost of his former self: his pallid, sallow features, drawn and exhausted; frightened, haunted eyes sunk beneath heavy brows; and his cropped, tufted hair struggling to regain its domain. Lieutenant Jack Carpenter, 8th Battalion, Royal Sussex Regiment, wounded in action on the Somme, 1st July 1916.

It seemed as though a gaping void had opened up between

the fearless, eager young man in spotless uniform who had strutted off so confidently to glory amid the cheers and flag-waving two years previously, and the gaunt, harrowed figure which now stood staring back at him from the mirror.

To think of himself now in that uniform seemed almost presumptuous. Likewise the recollection of those heady days was a hideous, capricious intrusion into the sanctuary he now sought and a hindrance to his bid for freedom from his own private hell. Instinctively he raised his hand to finger the gnarled, furrowed scar gashed across the right side of his head, gradually becoming camouflaged beneath the new growth of hair.

All at once his mind waded back into the frothing torrent of nightmare images and the cacophony of those final moments: the demonic shrieks of the shells as they screamed overhead, blasting open the earth with blistering thuds; the incessant, nauseating rattle of the unseen machine guns and the barbaric yells of men heaving and stumbling through the choking smoke, driven on by relentless fear. One could smell the fear, mingled with the broken earth, cordite and the stench of freshly mutilated flesh and entrails. A varied selection of grisly remnants of one-time human beings, smashed and ripped apart littered the pummelled, pockmarked ground.

The sound of Amy stirring in the bed suddenly and thankfully relieved him from this vile collage of death and carnage, which for months now would invade his mind time and time again. He stepped back lightly to the edge of the bed and stood gazing at this angel of mercy who had done so much to soothe him out of these frequent forays into depression, holding him back from the brink of complete insanity.

He studied the fine, regular features of her oval face, the tumble of soft, honey-blonde hair upon the pillow and the permanent hint of a childlike smile which played around her soft, pink lips. It had been that smile which had caught his attention the first time he had set eyes on her.

She had looked so efficient, so official and yet so delightfully charming in her neatly-pressed and starched, blue and white uniform, as she approached him from among the flurry of nurses and orderlies, waiting to usher in the latest consignment of wounded and dying from the Front.

What a contrast to the mass of human misery stuffed aboard the *SS Buckinghamshire*, which had lurched painfully and arduously across a choppy English Channel with its pitiful cargo of broken bodies and tormented souls.

# THE HOSPITAL

For most of the journey Jack had lain uncomfortably on a makeshift bunk in a dingy corner of what had previously been the dining saloon. His head had pounded like the guns at the Front, as he had drifted in and out of consciousness.

In the bunk next to his lay a burly Scots guardsman with his right shoulder completely shattered by a shell blast and whose blackened arm had already succumbed to gangrene. The man groaned and cursed endlessly throughout the crossing, cursing the ship, cursing the sea, cursing the army, the Hun, God and the world.

Opposite them lay a boy of little more than sixteen who, for the entire twelve hours on board, had moaned and wept incessantly, calling out for his mother. His whole upper body and head were swathed in bandages with tiny slits for his nose and mouth, which made him look like some grotesque parody of an ancient Egyptian mummy. He had been horribly burned and blinded by gas. Jack guessed the boy would not last long.

He had seen the devastating effects of mustard gas before. Not many of those caught in its insidious grasp ever survived. Not only did it burn the flesh and scorch out the eyes but once inhaled, it continued unseen its evil, hideous work on its victim, slowly but surely corroding the lungs until the poor beggar coughed and gagged his way into blessed oblivion.

As the vessel had rounded Spithead in the Solent and made its way up Southampton Water towards the docks, a Royal Army Medical Corps sergeant had ordered everyone to stand by, ready to be disembarked. There was a general groan of approval as those that could, heaved themselves to their feet. A refreshing draught of fresh air blew through the dank lower decks, helping to flush away the stench of stale blood, grime and seasickness.

For what seemed an eternity they waited patiently to be called or carried aloft and into the brilliant summer sunshine. They were carefully disembarked onto the dockside and from there transferred onto waiting hospital trains. These then ferried them on the final leg of their journey, a few miles back along the eastern side of the estuary to Netley, and to the specially-built railway halt behind the enormous edifice that was the Royal Victoria Hospital.

## The Hospital

The village of Netley lies nestled on the shores of Southampton Water and the great military hospital had been built there in the late 1850s and early 1860s, following the Crimean War. It was commissioned at the behest of dear old Queen Victoria herself, to care for wounded soldiers returning from their heroic exploits for queen and country in the far-flung reaches of the Empire. It had served the country well and now once more was answering the call to duty.

As the train eased its way to a stop, a dissonance of slamming doors, hurried footsteps and raucous shouts of instruction threatened to overwhelm Jack and exacerbate the pounding in his head.

After what seemed like another eternal wait, as one by one the casualties were taken off the train, Jack was finally helped out of the carriage by a grey-uniformed orderly. As he stepped unsteadily onto the little platform, his gaze was met by the sight of an immense, red-brick building, stretching a quarter of a mile left and right, standing like some enormous, palatial stately home amid its vast estate which ran down to the water's edge.

The orderly eased him gently into a wheelchair and began to push him along the crowded platform towards the entrance of the vast structure, which towered over this latest batch of arrivals, like some gigantic mother hen gathering unto herself so many thousands of chicks, like him.

Jack's head was spinning and thumping with every movement as he was wheeled towards the entrance. He felt sick again and wanted to lie down.

As they entered the megalithic building, the first things that struck him were the stark aroma of coal tar and disinfectant and the sound of brisk heels as they clicked officiously along shiny tiled floors. A regiment of nurses bustled this way and that, as they ushered their wounded charges to reception bays, wards and operating theatres.

And suddenly, there she was at his side, offering to take over from the orderly who was needed back at the train to help disembark further casualties.

'Here we are, Lieutenant; let me help you now. It's not far and we'll soon have you feeling more comfortable,' she said, smiling sweetly and with a genuine kindness in her voice, as she began to manoeuvre the wheelchair through a seemingly endless maze of corridors. Her gentle, reassuring tone, like that of some enchanting angel, echoed through his brain as they made their way among the hive of busyness into the bosom of this benign monster and an uncertain future.

Once or twice he nearly tipped out of the chair as the throbbing in his head and the bouts of giddiness assailed him and he lurched forward in pain. But this gentle soul reached out to steady him and ease him backwards into the chair with a strength that belied her petite stature.

'First of all we had better get you cleaned up a little and then one of the doctors will want to see you,' the angel said as they turned along yet another endless passageway.

Presently, he found himself in a sterile room painted in cream and green with high windows that let in broad shafts of light from the outside world. Along one wall stood a grim row of wooden chairs, some already occupied by a handful of 'walking wounded', whilst opposite sat a rather plump, unattractive woman with piercing, dark brown eyes and short dark curls tucked under her nurse's cap. She was dressed in a red and white, ill-fitting uniform and was shuffling various forms and papers on the desk in front of her.

The angel wheeled him towards this formidable-looking woman and suggested politely that the lieutenant needed to be seen quite urgently. The woman glanced up briefly as if to satisfy herself that this was indeed the case.

'Name, rank, number and regiment?' she rapped.

'Carpenter, Jack. Second Lieutenant. Er...A73...48...19...2...Royal Sussex,' he stuttered uncertainly.

'Where's your repatriation paper?' she continued, without an iota of sympathy, doubtless cultivated by the many thousands of wounded young men she had witnessed over the past two years and which had hardened her against any sense of normal human compassion.

Jack attempted to fumble his way into the left breast pocket of his grimy tunic but his hand would not do as he wanted it. The angel immediately came to his rescue, unbuttoning the pocket for him and pulling out the creased, stained piece of paper that the dragon required. The latter studied it briefly and jotted a few notes.

'Take him through to bay four, Nurse!' barked the woman, without even looking up from her desk.

They moved through a long room with small, curtained bays on either side. From them came the moans and even occasional screams of the poor blighters who were being examined; obviously the most pressing cases.

They wheeled into an empty bay and the angel drew a dull, green-coloured curtain across the entrance in order to lend a little in the way of privacy.

'Right, Lieutenant, let's get you onto this bed and clean you up,' she said. She popped her head beyond the curtain and called for an orderly to lend assistance. A middle-aged, rather pale-looking man entered the bay and smiled knowingly but not unpleasantly. Between them they tentatively eased Jack out of the wheelchair to a somewhat shaky standing position. Very carefully they peeled off his grubby, stained uniform and laid him onto the bed where the angel proceeded to sponge away the grime.

Although they had cleaned him up superficially at the casualty clearing station and then at the transit hospital in Boulogne, he still felt as though he were permanently caked in the blood and sweat of battle. He was, after all, still wearing the same uniform.

'Oh, you're not wearing your identity tag, Lieutenant,' observed the orderly casually. 'Is it in your uniform pocket, perhaps?'

'Er...I'm not sure. Sorry,' stumbled Jack. 'Maybe I lost it somewhere.'

The angel rummaged through Jack's uniform pockets but found nothing.

'Don't worry, Sir! It happens sometimes,' she said, reassuringly.

After his wash, the orderly helped him into a pair of hospital-issue, blue, starched pyjamas as they waited for a doctor to come and examine his wound.

Jack listened to the hubbub of voices and the groans and curses of wounded and dying men echoing around the cavernous room.

Presently the noise began to fade, as he felt himself gradually slipping away yet again into a state of semi-consciousness.

He had absolutely no idea how long he had lain there or what had happened to him during that time. He had been aware, just occasionally, of a blurred backdrop of muffled voices and fuzzy figures as they glided to and fro past the rectangles of light from the tall windows along the opposite wall. Once or twice he had a vague sense that somebody was leaning over him and thought he could hear a soft, kindly voice seemingly calling to him as if from the far end of a long, deserted street. He had struggled desperately to return the call, but in vain. Try as he might, no sound would come from his parched lips. It was just like a nightmare when you struggle helplessly to run from some unseen and threatening danger and yet your legs are sapped of strength and you cannot make any headway.

It was in fact nine days later that he finally emerged from his stupor. Quite suddenly and for no obvious reason, his eyes popped wide open, sensation gushed back through his body and at once his mind became sharp and clear. He wriggled to a half-sitting position and looked around his alien surroundings in a vain effort to find something familiar and comforting. He stared at the array of beds - some empty, others with men lying on them - and at the knots of nurses and orderlies busying hither and thither.

'Ah! So the sleeper awaketh!' came an unfamiliar, yet cheerful voice from his left hand side. Perched on the bed next to his sat a tall, gangling figure with a mop of sandy hair and a matching handlebar moustache, surmounting a row of glistening, white teeth. The man must have been about the same age as Jack and seemed to be one of those people who sported a permanent grin. He had the palest blue, brilliant eyes that almost sparkled when he spoke and even his voice radiated a sense of happy-go-lucky cheerfulness and bonhomie.

'It's all right, old man. You're in hospital. I must say, you're looking considerably better than when they wheeled you in here the other day after your op. My word you looked grim!

'Oh, sorry old chap! Pritchard-Jones, Second Lieutenant, Queen's Royals, by the way. And you're Carpenter, eh? Couldn't help but sneak a look at your notes when Sister wasn't around! Actually, she's not a bad sort,' he chuntered on. 'A bit starchy, but then aren't they all? The junior nurses, and even the orderlies, live in absolute dread of her though. In fact, even one or two of the doctors tend to cower in her presence!'

At first, Jack could only stare vacantly at his new-found companion but he soon began to warm towards this garrulous, happy fellow and to feel at ease in his presence. He managed to blurt out a few mumbled words of acknowledgement and greeting until Pritchard-Jones hailed a nurse and took obvious pride in announcing to her that his neighbour had finally regained consciousness.

'I say, Nurse, look! Our sleeping beauty has returned to the land of the living!'

'So, Lieutenant, how are we feeling today?' It was the clear, mellow voice of the kindly nurse who had wheeled him into this vast building. Jack recognised her with a start and managed to summon a weak smile at this gorgeous creature.

'Would you like to try to sit up properly?' she asked gently and began to ease him forward, plumping the pillows behind him.

'I'll tell Sister you're awake and she'll fetch Dr Haines-Webster to come and have a look at you.

'I must say, it's nice to see you looking brighter. Quite a worry you gave us, Sir!' And with that, she bustled away to find Sister.

'I say, old boy, a bit of all right, that one, don't you think? She's been keeping a careful eye on you ever since they brought you into the ward! You know I do believe she's taken a bit of a shine to you,' chuckled Pritchard-Jones, good-naturedly.

Jack forced a grin, sank back, closing his eyes again and hoped it might be true.

A few moments later a posse comprising the redoubtable Sister Truckett, Dr Haines-Webster and the blonde angel bristled down the ward towards him and halted at the end of his bed.

Haines-Webster was a man in his early sixties, with thinning grey hair, a bushy moustache, fluffy sideburns and a prematurely lined face. A renowned and brilliant military surgeon-major, he had learned his trade on the African battlefields of the Empire during the 80s and 90s. Rumour had it he had been at the infamous battle of Rourke's Drift; but no one dared ask him if it were true.

He stood erect to his full six feet two inches, as he looked down studiously on his patient, puffing on his ever-present curved pipe and exuding an air of complete and absolute authority.

'Well, Lieutenant, how are we feeling today, eh?' he asked in a brisk, business-like tone, as he plucked the notes from the end of Jack's bed and scanned them casually.

'A bit better, Sir, although my head's still thumping like hell.'

'Well, it will do, man, it will do! That was quite a lump you've had taken out of it! But it could have been a damn sight worse. I've taken far bigger chunks than that out of men!'

'That's comforting to know, Sir,' replied Jack, equally sardonically.

'Nurse, remove the dressing, will you?' ordered the surgeon-major and as the angel leaned across him, Jack exulted in the few seconds of feeling her close to him and catching the sweet scent of her presence as she cautiously and gently unwound the bandages swathed around his head.

Haines-Webster moved round to the side of the bed to make a closer examination of Jack's wound, prodding the boggy indentation gently with his fingers and turning Jack's head this way and that to obtain a better angle from which to inspect his handiwork of eight days previously.

A lump of shrapnel had lodged itself at a shallow angle in the right hand side of Jack's head just above the hairline. Incredibly it had not penetrated far and had caused only minor fracturing of his skull.

After a few incomprehensible mutterings and grunts, made even less intelligible by the permanent presence of the pipe clenched securely in the corner of his mouth, Haines-Webster finally stood back, folded his arms and looked directly at Jack.

'You're an extremely lucky man, Lieutenant. Another half an inch further over and you could have had your whole head smashed in! As it is, you've got away with just a nasty crack and a bit of a dent. You'll feel pretty rough for a bit but there's no permanent damage done! You're likely to get a few headaches for the next while, too, but a few months' rest and recuperation and we'll be able to send you back to the Front to re-join your regiment, good as new.

'We'll need to keep you here for a wee bit longer though, just to keep an eye on you.' And with that the surgeon-major turned swiftly on his heels and marched off purposefully down the ward, closely followed by Sister Truckett.

Jack watched them go and then became instantly aware of the angel, as she stood at the foot of his bed, smiling down at him.

'Now then, Lieutenant, let me put a fresh, clean dressing on for you.'

'What's your name, Nurse?' he ventured, as she leaned over him to re-dress his wound and he could indulge once more in the sweet smell of her closeness, feel the soft touch of her fingers deftly wrapping the bandage and relish the brush of her uniform against his cheek.

'Can't you read my badge? It's Nurse Timmons.'

'No, I mean your Christian name.'

'Now why on earth would you want to know that, Lieutenant?' she teased.

'Just curious,' he said.

'Well, if you must know, it's Amelia. But most people call me Amy.'

'Amy,' he muttered half to himself, closing his eyes. 'That's pretty...' With that he lay back, tired but contented and drifted once more into sleep.

*

The following morning the early sun streamed pleasantly into the long, echoing ward. It was only just six o'clock but the day staff had come on duty and Jack was roused by the murmur of voices, as patients gradually emerged from their slumbers and the nurses busied themselves, drawing back the curtains and preparing for the breakfast round.

He instinctively glanced over to greet his chirpy neighbour but the bed to his left stood empty. For a split-second Jack panicked but then relaxed again as he saw the ever-ebullient Pritchard-Jones at the far end of the high, vaulted ward, chatting and laughing with one of the orderlies and another patient. He lay back, relieved but then found himself, quite subconsciously, eagerly scanning the long room in hope of catching sight of the blonde angel. Was she on duty today? Had she been moved to another ward? Would he ever see her again? He looked and looked in vain.

'Breakfast, Lieutenant?' A voice suddenly interrupted his reverie.

He glanced up to see an orderly lowering a dark wooden tray with a plate of scrambled eggs and bacon onto his lap as he pulled himself up into a comfortable sitting position.

'Would you like some tea, Sir?' asked the orderly.

'Er…yes…yes please. Thank you,' stuttered Jack in reply, but only half attentively and still anxiously scouring the ward for any sign of that image of loveliness from the previous day. The orderly placed the mug of steaming tea onto the bedside cabinet and moved on to the next patient.

Jack continued looking up and down the ward. Some of the men were able to sit at the long tables running down the middle between the beds to eat their meals whilst others like himself, not yet able safely and comfortably to get up, remained in their beds.

Finally he resigned himself to the fact that she was not there and began to chomp at the eggs and rather fatty bacon on the tray in front of him; but after only a few mouthfuls he began to feel nauseous and his head started to throb once more. He slid back down into the bed, closed his eyes and sought to wait out the pain.

He must have drifted back into sleep for it was three hours later that he came to once more, to find Pritchard-Jones perched beside him shuffling a pack of playing cards as if waiting for Jack to wake up in order to offer him a game. His tray of uneaten breakfast had disappeared.

'Hello, old boy! How are you feeling today? Sorry I missed

you earlier but you seemed out for the count and I didn't want to disturb your beauty sleep!' chirped his neighbour.

Jack forced a wan smile and thanked Pritchard-Jones for his thoughtfulness.

'I say,' continued Pritchard-Jones, 'that rather pretty nurse was in here a while ago; you know, the one that's taken a shine to you! Wanted to know how you were. Said she was off duty and had to get the train into town. Something about having to visit her folks, I think she said.'

Jack smiled to himself gratefully. She had been to see him. She had asked after him. She had cared about him. And a beautiful, warm contentment flooded through his veins. It was a wondrous feeling of euphoria which, although only temporary, helped to subdue the sense of pain, frustration and ignominy that had hovered over him for the past days like some malevolent bird of prey.

During the next few days Jack found himself eagerly awaiting the arrival of Nurse Timmons. He could not seem to figure out any kind of regularity or routine as to when she was on duty, so in the end he gave up trying. But whenever a new shift of nurses appeared on the ward, he would look anxiously to see if Amy were among them.

Then finally, four days later, he spotted her. He felt his heartbeat quicken and a thrill of excitement shoot through his whole being. She looked even lovelier than he remembered the last time he had seen her.

By now the ward was completely full, with ever-increasing numbers of casualties pouring back from the Front and all the nursing staff were evidently very busy. Jack's gaze was riveted on Amy as he watched her tripping up and down the ward ministering to all and sundry.

Every so often he liked to think she glanced in his direction and threw him an affectionate smile; but perhaps it was just wishful thinking on his part. Nevertheless, he yearned for the opportunity simply to speak with her again and sought unsuccessfully for some pretext or other on which to call her over.

Presently he slid away once more into a deep but fitful sleep. He could only maintain wakefulness for relatively short periods. For his brain, still struggling from the insult of the trauma it had suffered, would once more assume complete command of his body, conquering any emotional longing or desire to stay awake and impose its dominance upon him. But far from finding a place of rest or healing, his dreams would merely serve to transport him back again to those final moments.

# NIGHTMARE

Since first light the company had been waiting, quietly apprehensive in their section of the trench. After the rain of the preceding days, the hot July sun was making its way confidently into a clear blue expanse and gleaming down upon a quarter of a million silent men-at-arms who waited patiently, crouched obediently in their positions dug across the French countryside and anticipating with growing fear and trepidation the shrill and ever more closely approaching whistle, which would catapult them over the top.

Jack wove his way calmly among the line of men, Sergeant-Major Frobisher a pace or two behind him, as they waited nervously, standing down from the fire step, and did his best to focus their minds on the task ahead and to strengthen any weak knees. During the endless months of preparation and training both here in France and back in England, Jack had grown to like and respect these young boys, who not only respected the badge that he wore but who also clearly put their faith in the man himself. He muttered quiet words of encouragement and assurance as he walked along and prayed that, above all, he would not let them down.

The whole of the previous night he had sat, cramped in the damp and dingy dugout, searching in vain for even just a moment's sleep. His mind went over and over his orders for the day, desperate that he forget not one detail and thereby 'let the side down'. He saw before him the faces of each of his men in turn and wondered to himself how many, if any, would come through the ordeal which lay before them. He even found himself articulating what he might write to the relatives of those for whom the coming dawn would prove to be their last.

*'Dear Mr and Mrs… It is with deepest regret that I must inform you… He died doing his duty… He was a brave soldier… He did not suffer…'*

And now he even found himself reciting the oft repeated words of the top brass, that the whole show was going to be a walkover. He could not think of much else to say.


Sergeant-Major Frobisher, a large, powerful man of about forty, standing well over six feet tall, with cropped brown hair and a thick, bushy moustache, was a career soldier who had joined the ranks as a boy. He had seen action in the Sudan and South Africa and had been in the thick of it in France since the opening shots of this bloody war. His hard, craggy face seemed to have aged prematurely but his cold, steely eyes showed no trace of fear and exuded an air of strength and confidence to those around him, both enlisted men and officers alike.

Jack had enormous respect for this giant rock of a man and felt eternally grateful to be lucky enough to have him as his company sergeant-major. He was the sort of individual that personified absolute steadfastness and possessed that rare aura of utter invincibility. If Sergeant-Major Frobisher's with us, Jack thought to himself, we'll be all right. And subconsciously he determined to stick close to him during the assault.

The sun climbed ever higher above the horizon bringing with it the promise of a glorious summer's day. After a week of unrelenting and merciless bombardment, the guns had fallen strangely silent; one could even detect the occasional mellow chirping of summer birds as if they were determined to defy and outdo the man-made thunder of the previous seven days and regain their rightful status as the heralds of beauty and joy to the surrounding countryside.

Jack turned round suddenly as he became aware of a muffled commotion some twenty yards back down the line behind him. One of the younger lads had evidently had an attack of sheer panic, vomited and was now clawing at the walls of the trench, sobbing that he would refuse to go when the order came. His mates had jumped on him immediately to quieten him and steady him. Jack pushed his way towards the boy who gazed up at him from the bottom of the trench; his face was ashen and his eyes were like those of some terrified, hunted animal. Beads of sweat broke out all over his forehead and his shaking hands looked limp and useless.

'It's all right, Sir,' ventured one of his friends to Jack, 'we'll take care of him.' Jack nodded quietly in assent as the men tried to encourage the boy to take another shot of rum and reassure him that he would be OK.

Jack glanced at his watch for the hundredth time. Two minutes to go. All along the line the vague, muted sound of men stirring and the jangle of tackle could be detected as each unit readied itself. Jack tugged at his lanyard and lifted his whistle to his dry, parched lips. He glanced towards Sergeant-Major Frobisher and, as had been previously arranged, nodded twice, as the signal to ready the men. The big, burly NCO, in his gravelly Scottish burr, calmly gave the order to fix bayonets, adding, 'And remember, lads, to stay together and hold the ruddy line!'

The swish of bayonets being withdrawn from sheaths and the click-clicking of them being fixed to rifle's end chorused down the trench.

One minute to zero hour.

The beautiful quiet of the morning was suddenly devastated as the artillery opened up from miles back, huge shells whizzing overhead to begin the creeping barrage.

Twenty seconds to go.

Jack pulled out his revolver from its brown, polished leather holster and flexed his hand around the butt. He became instantly aware that his palm was clammy.

Ten seconds to go. Six. Three. One.

He blew hard through his whistle but for an instant no sound would come. He panicked and then blew again with every ounce of breath in his body. Thankfully the shrill pipping sound rang out, along with that of a hundred others into the morning sunlight.

Jack hoisted himself up one of the ladders and scrambled

unceremoniously over and out of the trench, closely followed by his men. He glanced around momentarily to check they were all with him and as if to reassure himself that this was not some mad nightmare in which he was the only one racing alone into No Man's Land.

By now the noise of the guns was deafening, smoke was beginning to billow from all directions and the sun's rays were struggling to penetrate it. He heard himself barking out commands to his men to stay together and to hold the line. Just as they had been told to do, they tramped steadily and patiently through the summer grass and on towards the enemy lines.

But the 'piece of cake' they had been promised by the generals did not materialise.

Jack could hear the distinctive and all too familiar rattle of machine guns dead ahead and feel the slipstream of volleys of bullets as they zipped past him. Men began to drop into the lush grass. Men began to scream as their bodies were scythed and shredded by these merciless killing machines.

They said the German line had been pulverised. They said there wouldn't be anyone left in their trenches and dugouts. They said it would be a stroll. They had lied.

Jack felt suddenly trapped by fear and uncertainty. What should he do? This was not what was supposed to happen. This was not in the plans that they had so meticulously discussed and practised and learned by heart. This was not what they had trained for. Someone had changed the script without telling him and in turn he had not told his men.

A rush of guilt and anguish surged through his being and immersed him. He had let them down; these men whom he had come to love and admire and who in turn had come to put their trust in his ability to lead them. He had failed them.

All at once the reassuring boom of Sergeant-Major Frobisher's voice above the din rocked him out of his despondent musing.

'Stay together and keep bloody well moving forward!' he yelled. But amidst the confusion and cacophony and the smoke and the spouts of earth as they spewed into the air from exploding shells and in the face of the pitiless hail of lead, the line began to falter and become ragged; men lagged behind as they struggled in vain to keep up the momentum of advance. Strict orders had been given not to stop, even to attend to wounded comrades, but to push doggedly on. The objective had to be reached.

Jack continued to press forward, now almost oblivious to the mouth of hell into which he was surely entering. The scene around him was carnage beyond the vilest imagination. Bodies littered the pockmarked earth in grotesque contortions. Some still writhed and twitched as if in some kind of hideous seizure. Weird, guttural groans and cries of uncomprehending terror drained from them in a concerto of agony as, in an arena of horror, men wrestled with death. Blood spewed out of bodies in scarlet fountains. Men struggled futilely to pack their own entrails back into themselves as they oozed blue, purple and pink from ripped torsos onto the green grass. Men groped unseeing in the dirt trying to find legs blown off beneath them. Wild eyes stared terrifyingly from smashed and bloodied faces half shot away.

Jack was now driven not by some notion of glory and heroism but rather by a concoction of primeval fear and a desperate need for penitence for having let his men down and which must surely end in death.

He had absolutely no clue as to how far the company had advanced. He was not even certain they were still heading in the right direction. He could not say how many minutes or even hours had passed since they had stepped out of the safety of the trench. Time had become meaningless. He dared not look at his watch. He could not see how many of his men were still with him. Was he actually experiencing just a strange nightmare? Was this really happening? He strained his eyes to see through the fog of smoke and get some sort of bearing. He strained his ears to catch Sergeant-Major Frobisher's reassuring shouts close by. He could not hear him. Jack panicked again. And then, as though the noise and confusion of the battle reached a deafening crescendo, Jack felt suddenly transported into a place of quietness and rest. He felt a vague pain on the side of his head and a tingling fuzziness slowly envelop him. He suddenly had no idea where he was but it seemed as though he were lying in a meadow on a warm summer's day, the smell of fresh grass in his nostrils, the sun's soporific warmth gently soothing his brow and somewhere in the distance the faint hubbub of some busyness elsewhere. A warm trickle crept slowly down the contours of his face and he could taste a slight saltiness at the corner of his mouth. He stared up into the endless blue above, punctuated by blurred puffs of dirty white smoke sailing past him high overhead. And then he drifted gently into a long, black tunnel.

*

## Nightmare

For fourteen hours Jack lay unconscious in No Man's Land. The shell had exploded so close that he had not even heard the bang or felt the impact of the blast or the shard of burning shrapnel which had embedded itself into his right temple. As night had begun to descend across the battlefield to bring down the curtain on the first act of this sickening drama, the chill of the evening had wrested Jack back to consciousness. His mouth and throat felt dry and sore. He began to shiver and his head throbbed as if someone inside was hammering to get out. Involuntarily he went to lift his hand to touch the side of his head which hurt so much but found that the hand would not respond to his command. He tried again. Nothing. Suddenly aware of lying on his back, he tried to move his body and turn onto his side. Nothing happened. Jack panicked. His mind was a blur and he became frighteningly confused and disorientated. Where was he? Why could he not move? He opened his mouth to call for help but no sound came out. Was this simply just another dream? What was happening to him? He lay staring up at the sprinkling of stars which hung in the dark canopy above, as he tried desperately to make some sort of sense of this weird existence in which he found himself.

All at once he was aware of sounds and movements around

him. He could hear the pitiful moans and desperate calls of others like himself, trapped in this wilderness and unable to help themselves. Figures in the darkness were scurrying here and there. These were the medics and stretcher-bearer teams, as they ventured out under cover of night to retrieve their broken comrades and haul them back to the forward dressing stations tucked behind the lines. Jack vaguely sensed a dark shadow kneeling over him and gentle fingers delicately inspecting the grisly, indented gash on the side of his head.

'Take it easy, Lieutenant; we'll have you out of here in no time,' came a comforting voice. Jack tried in vain to speak.

'Here, drink this,' continued the anonymous figure and he poured a little water from a canteen onto Jack's cracked lips. Jack gulped it down thankfully and greedily and coughed as the cool liquid slipped down the wrong way. Next the man very cautiously swathed Jack's head in a field dressing and then with the aid of his partner eased him onto a stretcher.

As they carefully picked their way among the corpses and shell holes back to the lines, every jolt sent bolts of searing pain through Jack's head. The pain became unbearable. Nausea engulfed him. He creased his eyes tightly in an effort to shut out the merciless hammering in his brain. A few moments later he passed out once more.

The forward dressing station to which Jack was brought was little more than a small bunker dug into the side of a low grassy embankment and reinforced with a few heavy timbers, one of many such hastily-erected emergency first aid posts set up in the immediate aftermath of the bloodbath. Inside the fetid, dimly lit 'room' two dozen or so men lay on stretchers side by side. Some groaned in pain; others wept; some were eerily silent. A strange brew of earth, cordite, blood and iodine filled the air.

As night once more gave way to day the rumble of the guns started up again. Exhausted medics and orderlies shuffled constantly in and out. Now and then one of the stretchers would be carried away only to be replaced with a fresh victim. Chaos seemed to be the order of the day, for now the full horror of the previous twenty-four hours was becoming ever more apparent. It would become known as the worst day ever experienced in the history of the British Army. It would become infamous as one of the greatest military blunders of all time. It would become a byword for pointless slaughter. It would become known simply as 'The Somme'.

In the early afternoon Jack was examined by one of the medics. His wound was superficially cleaned and a fresh dressing applied in place of the blood-soaked bandage in which he had lain for so many more hours. Throughout this time he had ebbed and flowed in and out of consciousness. Now at last he was to be sent further back behind the lines to a casualty clearing station.

Together with a number of other stretcher cases he was unceremoniously loaded onto an old, heavy farm wagon. A young corporal from the Medical Corps took charge of the unwieldy cart, which was pulled by two huge, plodding shire horses. After a rough couple of miles negotiating muddy, rutted tracks and what seemed like an eternity later, they finally came to a halt outside a dilapidated barn attached to the remains of a once pretty and thriving farmhouse.

The men were unloaded and taken into the barn where bales of straw lining the walls acted as makeshift bunks. The place was already overflowing with the wounded. As this new batch arrived, a medical officer came over to inspect them; he looked drawn, pale and utterly exhausted. He, too, had been fooled by the lie that the battle was going to be a 'cakewalk' and that he need only expect to treat a handful of casualties.

He gave orders for Jack's wound to be washed again and re-dressed before he was moved on yet further behind the lines.

Along with some three dozen others, Jack was crammed into a London omnibus which had been requisitioned and brought out to the Front to help the war effort. Once everyone had been loaded on board, the engine coughed into life, the driver, a sergeant from the Royal Engineers, crunched the obstinate gears into action and the heavy-laden, makeshift ambulance trundled on its way.

Throughout the bumpy journey the men were accompanied by three Queen Alexandra nurses in their grey and white uniforms. These noble women of middle class families had gallantly turned their backs on their comfortable lives and, like so many others, had taken up the call to come to their country's aid in its hour of need, even to volunteer to come and serve at the Front. All through the journey they flitted amongst their charges, ministering to their needs and trying heroically to bring words of comfort and solace.

After four painful hours bumping through country lanes and damaged roads, the ambulance pulled up outside a modest-looking hotel in the centre of Boulogne. Once a pretty, bustling port, the town now resembled a gigantic army barracks. British military personnel swarmed everywhere; military vehicles rumbled through the cobbled streets and every park and patch of open space had been transformed into a city of tents. Since this British 'invasion', L'Hôtel de la Gare had been requisitioned as a transit hospital by the military authorities and it was here that the ambulance's curious passengers were to be disembarked.

Because of the vast numbers streaming back from the battlefield, the temporary wards were already overflowing and yet more tents had been hurriedly erected in the grounds of the hotel. It was to one such tent that Jack was taken on a stretcher, although he knew little about it, since he was still only semiconscious.

During the hours that followed and his occasional forays into wakefulness out of the darkness which seemed to enfold him, he was intermittently aware of people around him, vague, incoherent exchanges between them and occasional sensations of someone touching his head.

The following day he found himself once more on the move. Because of the congestion created by the dreadful and unanticipated fallout from the battle, the decision was hastily made to evacuate as many of the casualties as was feasible back to Blighty as speedily as possible. All military hospitals throughout the land had been placed on high alert and unofficially warned to expect the worst.

Jack lay on his stretcher on the quayside for three hours, together with a thousand others patiently waiting their turn for the next hospital ship to tie up.

By midday the *SS Buckinghamshire* had cast off and pulled slowly out of Boulogne harbour to make her way, homeward bound, across the Channel.

# RETURN TO SANITY

Jack was roused from his slumber by the soft voice of the angel.

'Lieutenant. Lieutenant. Would you like some tea?'

And as his eyes flickered open to give relief from the torment he had been reliving, he felt a euphoric rush of wellbeing course through his body. There she was, as lovely as ever, looking down at him, still smiling that warm, gentle smile.

Eagerly he grinned back at her and struggled to lever himself up into a sitting position.

She handed him a welcome mug of hot tea and checked to see that he could handle it steadily without spilling any.

'Thank you. That's very kind,' said Jack and desperately hoped she might stay a while and talk with him.

'Er...I haven't seen you recently,' he said clumsily, and immediately felt rather foolish for having done so.

'Well, I have had two days off and went home to visit my parents. But I'm most pleased to see you looking so much better now, Lieutenant. And look! You can move your arm again properly!'

'Please call me Jack,' he blurted out.

'You'll get me into trouble with Sister. We are not supposed to address patients by their Christian name!'

'I won't let on if you don't,' he smiled. 'It can be our secret! Sister need never know!'

'You cannot keep secrets from Sister. I think she has some sort of sixth sense. She seems to know everything about everyone and certainly everything that goes on in the ward!'

'Do your parents live very far away?' he ventured, partly to discover more about this exquisite creature but also to keep her close to him for as long as possible.

'No, not far at all. Just across the other side of the water in fact.'

And with that their conversation seemed to come to an end. Jack couldn't think what else to say and as she glanced around slightly anxiously, he guessed he should allow the poor girl to carry on with her duties.

'Thanks again for the tea, Nurse…er…I mean, Amy. Perhaps I'll see you tomorrow,' he said.

'Perhaps,' she smiled and continued on her way.

Jack sipped his tea and for the rest of the evening felt rather exultant.

Two days later he was well enough to get out of bed and be taken to sit in the grounds of the hospital. It was a warm, inviting, sunny morning as the orderly wheeled him along the echoing corridors and out into the bracing sea air. He positioned the wheelchair carefully on a lawn beneath a broad, spreading fir tree where Jack could look out onto the water and observe the comings and goings of the busy port further upstream.

'Will that be all right, Sir?' asked the orderly, as he wrapped a blanket over Jack's lap.

'Yes. Thank you. That's first rate. I shall be absolutely fine here.'

'I will collect you again in an hour or so to take you back in for lunch. Are you sure you will be all right now?'

'Yes, really, I'm fine. Thank you.'

Jack was grateful of the opportunity simply to savour some time away from the noise of the busy ward, to reflect a little in the relative peace of the outdoors in the kind, late summer sunshine and to gaze at the stunning panorama that lay before him. Beyond the fringes of the hospital's sweeping grounds, Southampton Water stretched blue and calm. Vessels of various kinds continued to ply up and down and Jack could not help but notice how many obviously hospital ships were regularly entering the estuary. Further still, he could see quite clearly the far side of the water and the dark silhouette of the New Forest skyline.

As he gazed across, he found his thoughts once more, as they had done a thousand times in the past few days, turning to Nurse Timmons. Amy. She had mentioned that she lived on the other side of the water. Perhaps he was looking even now directly towards her home. What sort of a home would it be? What would her parents be like? Did she have any brothers or sisters? Jack found a myriad of such inane questions teeming through his mind until finally he took a conscious grip of himself and told himself not to be so foolish.

As a common antidote to hope, so as not to be disappointed, he began trying to convince himself that Nurse Timmons was not the slightest bit attracted to him and that her kindness and beautiful smile were merely well-honed, professional attributes with which she charmed all the patients here. He was a complete fool to entertain such romantic notions about her.

Besides, a smashing-looking girl like that probably had many admirers, especially within this male-dominated environment. And without doubt she was already walking out with one of the young doctors.

But whilst in his mind he sought to embrace these logical and rational thoughts, in his heart he was unashamedly in love.

All of a sudden he was jolted from his daydreaming by the chirpy voice of Pritchard-Jones.

'Hello, old boy! Somebody said you'd been brought out for a bit of air. How are you feeling today? I missed you at breakfast. Slipped off to have a chat with that poor bugger they brought in yesterday. You know, the Anzac chap who came in with both legs shot away.'

From within his stupor, Jack had been vaguely aware of some disturbance the previous night, as yet another victim was wheeled into the ward having undergone emergency surgery to have the ragged remnants of both shattered limbs amputated. Apparently the poor man had moaned through most of the night as the ether began to wear off and the agony started to set in. Nurses had fussed around him from hour to hour, monitoring the desperate man's progress and by morning he had finally quietened through a cocktail of morphine and exhaustion.

'Yes, I thought it would be nice to have a change of scenery and it's a pleasant day,' said Jack. 'I've been sitting here watching the traffic on the water. Countless vessels have been going up and down, though mostly up, towards the docks. Yet more casualties, I suppose. There seems to be no end to them. What the hell must be happening over there?'

'I know what you mean,' replied his companion. 'Every day the lists in the paper get longer and longer. The whole show must be a bloody disaster.'

For a moment or two the pair of them sat in a subdued and sombre silence.

'Anyway, old boy, how's progress with that dishy little nurse you're after?' ventured Pritchard-Jones, returning to his normal, jovial self, in an attempt to lighten the atmosphere.

Jack felt himself blush.

'What do you mean?' he replied, and shuffled his position in a vain attempt to hide his discomfiture.

'Oh, don't play coy with me, you randy old goat! It's pretty damned obvious to everyone on the ward that you've fallen for her!'

Jack squirmed and blushed further. Had it really been so

obvious?

'Very well, I admit I do find her most attractive,' he conceded.

'Don't feel apologetic about it, old boy! She's a cracking little wench!' Pritchard-Jones continued to tease him and, after a slight pause, 'I could even take a fancy to her myself!'

'Don't you dare!' retorted Jack. 'She's mine!'

'Oh! Possessive, too!' Pritchard-Jones pressed on.

Finally Jack capitulated under this incessant barrage of good-natured banter.

'All right, you win, you bastard!' he conceded. 'Yes, I do fancy her. I think she's the loveliest girl I've ever come across.'

'And have you told her so?' his friend challenged.

'I'm not sure I could. And in any case, what on earth would a pretty thing like that want with a broken wreck like me? Let's face it, she must have come across a thousand blokes in this place, all of whom have taken a fancy to her. No doubt she is already walking out with one of the docs anyway.'

'Well, you won't know for sure until you ask her, will you? If I were you, I'd get my bid in quick, old boy.

'Anyway, I had better be off. I promised to play cards with that mob in F ward at twelve. Toodle-pip old chap!'

And with that he sauntered off back indoors, whistling cheerily. As Jack watched him go, he smiled and wondered how this roguish yet charming fellow always managed to be so cheerful.

He also wondered what was actually wrong with him. He did not appear to have any obvious signs of wounds and he had never mentioned anything about injuries, where he had been in the fighting, or even how long he had been in the hospital. A bit of a mystery, thought Jack.


And so the days passed. On occasion, Jack was able to while away the hours outside in the soothing warmth of a late August sun. He was grateful of the opportunity to be wheeled around the expansive grounds of the giant hospital and to enjoy the beautiful vistas across the water. Late summer flowers blossomed in the thoughtfully tended borders and the smell of fresh mown grass wafted in the breeze accompanied by the salt air drifting off the water.

Gradually his strength began to return and within another week or so he was able to walk unaided, albeit a little unsteadily, as he learned to regain his balance and coordination once more. The pain in his head lessened, too, and Haines-

Webster was pleased with his progress; and even more pleased with his own handiwork.

Jack had thought long and hard since his conversation with Pritchard-Jones and, ever more frequently, allowed himself the luxury of entertaining notions of finding out from Amy whether or not she was already 'spoken for'. He lived for the moments each day of catching sight of her as she went about her work, and finding the smallest of excuses to talk with her as often as he could. He no longer cared what others might think of him. The gentle softness of her voice thrilled him and he dreamt most nights of her enchanting, sensuous smile.

# CHEAP DAY RETURN

With a double pip from its whistle, the train puffed out of Woolston Station and chuffed on its way towards the centre of Southampton. Jack sat back in his seat, gazing out of the window and could see the giant shipbuilding works as the train now headed across the river and into the heart of the metropolis. His heart was pounding with excitement and his head spinning with exhilaration. For opposite him sat Amy, wrapped in her nurse's cape and looking as adorable as ever.

He could hardly believe it was really happening and kept having to convince himself that this was not just some exotic fantasy, playing out in his head.

Only with the cunning help of Pritchard-Jones had he managed to pull off such a ruse. Against all the odds he had convinced the steely Sister Truckett that he desperately needed to do some shopping for his elderly mother, whose birthday it soon was. He persuaded her that he felt well enough to venture to the shops in Southampton and that the outing would surely aid his convalescence. However, he would, of course, need some assistance. And then came the best bit. Sister agreed that, if she were willing, Nurse Timmons may accompany him, but it would have to be on her day off.

'We are far too busy on the wards to allow nurses to go swanning off whilst on duty just because young upstart officers want to buy birthday presents for their mothers!' she clucked, with just the hint of a twinkle in her eye and almost the suspicion of a smile on her dour face.

'How big is the town?' Jack enquired, as the train rattled on its way. 'I've not been here before, except to the docks, of course, when I was brought back from France.'

'Well, it's nowhere as grand as London but it is a fair size for a provincial town. I'm afraid I'm not sure how many people live here,' Amy confessed.

Jack took in the view of West Bay as the train slowed into the station and screeched to a halt. Whistles blew and doors slammed open along the platform. 'Southampton West! Southampton West! All change for Waterloo!' wailed a voice as Jack and Amy alighted and mingled with the crowds making their way to the exit.

As they came out onto the street, Jack stood awhile just to

absorb the scene of busy normality and soak up the bustling atmosphere of the place. People hurried and scurried about their daily lives. Uniformed men promenaded in the bracing salt air of this famed maritime town - many, like him, with a girl at their side. Red and cream trams hurtled past amid the delivery vans and wagons. And even a few automobiles coughed their way along the busy street. It was a bright, crisp, autumnal day and Jack felt quite uplifted.

'It is a little bit of a walk up to where the shops are,' said Amy, as they made their way out of the railway station precincts and up the long, gentle climb of Commercial Road towards the town centre. They wandered through the greenery of Watts Park, named after one of the town's famous sons, Isaac Watts, and from there continued on, passing the imposing façade of the town's Grand Theatre on the corner of Windsor Terrace with billboards advertising the latest music hall show to hit the South and then into Southampton's main artery, Above Bar Street.

Turning right, they strolled along in the October sunshine, glancing in the windows of the shops which began now to spring up with increasing regularity as they approached the heart of the town.

Finally, they found themselves standing before the medieval town gate known as The Bargate. Jack looked admiringly at the grey, stone monolith and the remnants of the old town walls radiating from it to left and right.

'Shall we go on down to the High Street?' suggested Amy. 'Now you must tell me what you have in mind to buy for your mother and then I can think which shops we might visit.'

'I'm afraid I'm not much good at coming up with ideas. What would you suggest?'

'Would she like some scent or jewellery or perhaps some pretty porcelain?' ventured Amy.

Jack considered for a moment or two.

'Possibly some jewellery. I'm sure she would appreciate that,' he said at last.

'In that case let us turn down here. I know a fine little jeweller's shop down at the far end.' And with that she steered him into East Street. A couple of hundred yards further on they found themselves standing outside a neat and welcoming little shop displaying an array of fine gold and silver, including rings sparkling with diamonds and other precious stones. Jack stared thoughtfully in the shop window searching for some pretty piece to catch his eye.

'What do you think she might enjoy?' enquired Amy.

'Well, how about a locket and a chain?' he replied. 'Look they have some there at the back.'

'Let's go in and look at them then,' smiled Amy, and almost bundled him through the door.

They were served by a courteous, middle-aged man with a head of thick, dark hair and bushy eyebrows who clearly knew his trade and could tell them every detail they might possibly wish to know about the various lockets and chains he had on offer. After much discussion and comparison, and with Jack constantly deferring to Amy's opinion, he finally selected a delicate, silver locket, engraved with the form of a crocus, attached to an equally delicate and pretty chain.

'I'll take this one, please. I'm sure my mother will adore it,' said Jack.

'A very good choice, Sir,' replied the jeweller. He carefully placed the item in a little, silver-coloured box and wrapped it in brown paper. Money changed hands and the transaction was completed.

Ten minutes later Jack and Amy were making their way at a leisurely pace back towards the Bargate, Jack's parcel safely tucked inside his greatcoat pocket.

'Nurse Timmons,' he said, with forced irony, 'may I invite you for afternoon tea?'

'That would be delightful, Lieutenant Carpenter,' replied Amy, with equal irony in her voice.

'Where would you care to go?' he asked.

'There's a charming little tea shop at the end of the High Street down by the pier. I sometimes go there with my mother whenever we come into town to shop. And they serve excellent toasted teacakes.

'But are you sure you can manage to walk that far, though?' she asked with genuine concern. 'I must not tire you out. Sister would not be pleased if I took you back to the hospital worn out and exhausted!'

'I'll be fine,' Jack reassured her, relishing every moment of this beautiful Indian summer afternoon in the company of this heavenly creature.

They found a quiet table by the window of the quaint, yet very refined tea shop, which afforded them an uninterrupted view of the upper reaches of Southampton Water. The vast docks were now crammed with countless ships of every description either tied up or lying at anchor and smaller craft buzzing between them.

'This is quite an impressive town, I must say,' said Jack.

'Well, it has everything one could want, I suppose - shops and entertainments and so on,' Amy replied, 'but I prefer living over there in the Forest.' And she threw a glance through the window across the water to the low, tree-lined horizon on the other side. 'That really is a beautiful place,' she said. 'You should visit it someday, Jack.'

'Perhaps you might take me there one day and show it me,' he said, and then felt immediately foolish for being so presumptuous. Fortunately, he was rescued from his embarrassment by the timely arrival of the waitress.

'A pot of tea for two and some of your delicious teacakes, please,' Amy ordered.

'Yes, Madam.'

'I…I'm sorry, I didn't mean to…' started Jack.

'I'd be pleased to take you out to the Forest, Jack. It is so lovely there and particularly at this time of year when the trees begin to turn such vibrant colours. I often go for long walks when I'm home, through the woods and across the heath. I'm sure you would love it.'

Jack was grateful to her for putting him at his ease once more and as he glanced up at her gratefully, he was hypnotised once again by the magic of her smile.

Presently the tea and cakes arrived on blue and white fine china crockery and for some moments they sat quietly as they sipped the welcome tea and made short work of the cakes. They were indeed first class teacakes, particularly bearing in mind the difficulties and shortages of wartime.

'Would you like another cup of tea?' asked Amy, holding up the teapot.

'Oh, yes. Yes, please. Thank you.'

She poured them another cup each and they continued to sit in silence for a while against the backdrop of muffled voices of other guests and the occasional chink of bone china cups and saucers.

'I am so glad you managed to find something for your mother,' Amy at last broke the silence. 'Do tell me about her. I'm sure she is very special.'

Jack fidgeted slightly.

'Well, she's just fairly ordinary, I suppose,' he said. 'You know, just like everyone else's mother. But then, yes, everybody's mother is special, isn't she?'

'Does she live far away?'

'Yes, quite a long way. Over in Kent.'

'And what about your father, Jack. What does he do?'

Jack hesitated slightly, and then said, 'I never really knew my father. He died when I was very young. I…I don't have any clear recollection of him at all.'

'Jack, I am so sorry. I did not wish to embarrass you. Please forgive me for being so insensitive. It was quite rude of me.'

'No, no. It's all right. Please don't apologise. You haven't embarrassed me. Please, tell me about your parents.'

Amy tilted her head slightly to one side, glanced upwards and smiled thoughtfully for a moment, holding her teacup between both hands.

'Well, they live over in the Forest, as you know, in a little village called Bucksleigh. Papa is the rector of the parish. They're both very sweet. And well respected in the village, too, I think.'

'Do you have any brothers or sisters?' asked Jack.

'Just one brother: Richard. He's a couple of years older than me. He's serving in the Royal Navy so we don't see a great deal of him. But he writes when he can. Mama worries about him terribly, of course, but I think he is a lot safer at sea than at the Front. Oh! I'm sorry! That sounds rather callous, doesn't it?'

'No, not at all. We need our navy, just as much as we need

our chaps at the Front. I'm sure your brother is doing a splendid job.'

A glance at her watch prompted Amy to suggest they had better start making their way back to the railway station.

'We don't want to risk the wrath of Sister!'

They sauntered back up the High Street, once more through the medieval Bargate and along Above Bar Street until they reached Watts Park. Skirting the park this time, they made their way via West Park Road and Blechynden Terrace to reach the station with ten minutes to spare.

The afternoon sun was steadily seeping away and the autumn chill began to permeate the air once more. Jack was beginning to feel quite tired now and was grateful as they clambered into the warmth of the carriage and settled down for the short journey back to Netley.

They talked little during the return trip, commenting only on various landmarks as the train clattered past.

It was almost dark as they alighted from the train at the hospital halt and Amy ushered her patient back to the ward. The eagle-eyed Sister Truckett had duly noted their arrival with approval.

'Well, Nurse Timmons, how did he do?' she enquired with a

knowing look.

'Oh, very well, thank you Sister. I think the sunshine and the fresh air has done him the world of good,' replied Amy.

Jack had thoroughly relished his afternoon out and, during the days which followed, thought of little else, reliving every moment of the excursion. He kept reciting their conversations over and over in his mind, desperately hoping he had not inadvertently made a complete idiot of himself or embarrassed himself too much.

With each day that passed his fitness was returning and he often went for long walks around the extensive grounds of the hospital. Sometimes he would stand for hours staring out across the water, listening to the waves gently lapping on the quiet shore beneath him. Glancing to his left, he could follow the clear, jagged outline of the Isle of Wight, as it stood guard across the Solent at the entrance to Southampton Water. And to his right he could see the silhouettes of the town skyline and the chaos of ships crowding the harbour.

Directly in front of him, across the three-quarter or so mile stretch of water, lay the Forest and with that came the excitement of the memory of Amy's invitation to take him there one day, to share with him the beauty of the place that she clearly loved so much. He hoped it had not been one of those polite but idle proposals people so often make – well-meant and genuine at the time but actually of no substance and soon forgotten. Almost subconsciously, he schemed as to how he might remind Amy of her suggestion in order to ensure he could spend more time with her.

On other occasions Jack would sit in the quietness of the hospital chapel, which was set into the very centre of the colossal building. Attendance at the regular Sunday services held there for both staff and patients was expected, if not obligatory, for those physically able, but he preferred the simplicity of a visit once or twice a week, just to be alone with his own thoughts and musings. Occasionally he would even wonder whether he should pray. He was not quite convinced if the Almighty would hear him, but he guessed it could do no harm.

After one such visit he ventured nonchalantly over to an area of the hospital which was only rarely mentioned and then either disparagingly or in hushed tones and with a certain air of suspicion. It was known simply as D Block.

As he approached this outpost, set apart from the main

hospital complex and tucked away from view beyond a cluster of pine trees, he witnessed a curious and deeply disturbing sight.

A patient, dressed in the standard blue hospital uniform, was crouching at the corner of the building and looking around furtively. Jack glanced about him to see whom the man was either observing or attempting to avoid; he saw no one. Suddenly the man leapt out from his 'hiding place' and began strutting up and down along the path which fronted the building, yet at the same time shaking his head violently every few seconds and swinging his right arm like a bowler 'winding up' his bowling arm at cricket practice.

This strange behaviour continued for some minutes and every now and then the poor fellow would let out a succession of bizarre, animal-like noises and dribble down the front of his tunic. Jack was sickened and appalled. He wondered how or why this pathetic, crazed figure could be permitted to wander about, apparently unsupervised, when an orderly suddenly appeared from the main entrance.

'There you are, William! Now you know you are not allowed to be out here, don't you? Come on, let's get you back indoors. Doctor Shelcross is waiting to examine you.' And with that he gently, yet firmly, ushered William back into the bosom of D Block.

'You poor blighter,' muttered Jack.

He had heard many anecdotes, of course, about blokes suffering from what was commonly referred to as shell shock and had even witnessed at the Front, men who 'cracked' under the strain of fighting and who would dissolve into uncontrollable seizures of panic. Usually they would either be 'straightened out' by their company sergeant-major and returned to duty or, in a very few cases, be shipped back behind the lines. However, he had never witnessed first-hand, this kind of human degradation.

Officially there was no such condition as shell shock. Any man displaying symptoms of fear or panic was considered by the army to be a malingerer and branded a coward. This view was impressed upon all officers, who were naturally expected to uphold and reinforce any edict from the General Staff. The sight of this sad individual convinced Jack otherwise.

Later in the day Jack spoke to Pritchard-Jones about what he had experienced.

'Oh yes; didn't you know about the infamous D Block? It's where all the basket cases go for so-called therapy. Not quite sure what they do to the poor chaps but from what I've heard, it sounds more like torture than therapy. Apparently they give them electric shocks and all sorts. Poor beggars.'

For several days Jack was haunted by what he had seen and by what Pritchard-Jones had told him. He was incredulous that human beings could be treated so appallingly and within him a seed of anger took root.

Three weeks after his day out to Southampton, Jack knew for certain that the Good Lord had looked upon him favourably and answered his prayers. Haines-Webster had pronounced him well enough to be discharged and prescribed a further three months' convalescence leave before returning to his regiment.

This good news and Jack's general feeling of wellbeing as he continued to recuperate were, however, mixed with a sense of alarm, as he realised he would no longer be seeing Amy.

He was anxious to speak to her on the last day before his discharge. He had no idea what he might say to her but somehow he had to let her know what he felt for her. He could not simply walk away. And in any case, where was he going to go?

Once again the angel came to his rescue.

'So you're leaving us, Jack! Sister Truckett told me the good news when I came on duty. You must be pleased. And I hear they have granted you some sick leave before returning to your regiment.'

'Yes, apparently…,' he started.

'I suppose you'll go home to your mother, will you?' she enquired gravely.

'Well, I haven't given it a great deal of thought yet. I did wonder about finding some rooms in Southampton and staying down here for a while. I would quite like to acquaint myself with the area a little more.'

'Why don't you come and stay with us over at Bucksleigh for a few days? Just until you find somewhere, I mean. I'm sure my parents would not object. The Rectory is quite large and we have lots of room. In fact, I'm certain my parents would be delighted to feel they could 'do their bit' to help with the war and support a serviceman!'

Her words rang through Jack's brain like a peal of joyous celebration.

'That would be…er…absolutely…splendid,' he stammered, 'if you're sure it will suit your mother and father.'

'Of course. I will speak to them tonight when I return home. I have a day off tomorrow so I will come and collect you in the morning and we can catch the train into Southampton. We can then take the ferry over to Hythe and either walk or take the omnibus up to Bucksleigh.'

That night saw Jack sleep the happiest and dreamiest sleep of his life.

# THE FOREST

By eleven o'clock the following morning Jack and Amy were once more walking through the busy streets of Southampton, making their way to the ferry terminal next to the Royal Pier at the bottom of the High Street.

Jack had been duly discharged at eight thirty from Netley Hospital and had collected the necessary papers from Sister Truckett. He thanked her and the other nurses and orderlies for their help and care, said his 'goodbyes' to his compatriots on the ward and jaunted cheerfully out into the blue-sky day which fitted his mood perfectly.

As arranged, Amy was standing at the railway halt to meet him. For the first time since he had known her, she was not wearing the rather starchy, officious blue of her nurse's uniform. She was dressed in a long, elegant and fashionable burgundy coat with a black, fur-trimmed collar, a neat, pale cream cloche hat and laced ankle boots. She smiled as he approached and it was all he could do to prevent himself from taking her in his arms and kissing her.

'You look lovely,' he said. 'I have never seen you out of uniform before!' On their previous outing together, Sister Truckett had insisted that Amy wear her nurse's uniform and cape, despite it being her day off.

'Just in case...' she had said. 'He is our patient and we are responsible for him!'

'And you look very smart, in your uniform,' Amy countered and they both laughed. The hospital had supplied Jack with a freshly laundered uniform to replace the tatters in which he had arrived.

The now-familiar train journey passed quickly and the walk from the railway station to the ferry took half an hour at a leisurely pace. Jack felt elated. The sun looked down on them from a deep azure sky, the faces of people they passed in the street seemed to smile at them, while the birds in the park seemed to have delayed their winter departure in order to serenade them. And the war seemed a million miles away.

As they approached the ferry, Amy went immediately to purchase two tickets for the crossing while Jack gazed out upon the mighty port, humming with the busyness of another working day. In the middle distance he spotted what he assumed must be the ferry, ploughing its way through the grimy water towards the landing stage. As it drew closer he could make out the name *Hotspur* emblazoned on the bow of the red and white paddle steamer, so named since a forbear of the Percy family, who owned the ferry company, had been immortalised by the great Bard as 'Harry Hotspur'.

A gangway was slid into place to allow a knot of passengers to disembark and fresh passengers to clamber aboard. Jack and Amy found a seat aft and Jack exulted in the sunshine and the invigorating breeze upon his face as the *Hotspur* plip-plopped its way back across the estuary.

The village of Hythe sits about a third of the way down the western fringe of Southampton Water and acts as a local centre and natural link to the town for the handful of communities sprinkled across its hinterland.

'Hythe. That's an unusual name,' observed Jack. 'Does it have some sort of meaning?'

'I believe the name comes from an ancient word for 'hard', since the village grew up around a landing place for boats coming up the estuary,' Amy informed him. 'Then, during the Middle Ages, vessels which were too large to land their cargoes directly in Southampton, used to drop anchor in the estuary and the boatmen of Hythe would bring the goods ashore.'

Jack smiled as he noted Amy's evident enthusiasm in passing on her knowledge and he had to admit he was impressed by what she seemed to know.

'By the eighteenth century,' she continued, 'all kinds of ships were being built in the village. And the first mention of a ferry dates from fifteen hundred and something! But it's probable that some sort of link to Southampton existed even before that, right back to when the village was founded.'

'Well, Nurse Timmons. You are clearly a most learned historian!' teased Jack.

'Oh, I love history! I remember we once had to do a project at school all about the history of our local area. It was great fun and really interesting. That's how I know these things!'

Once more Jack smiled at this divine creature and wished he could hug her and tell her how much he adored her.

Twenty minutes or so after leaving the grand Royal Pier in Southampton, the *Hotspur* tied up alongside the somewhat humbler, wooden Hythe Pier. Jack and Amy disembarked under the watchful eye of the ferry's bo'sun who politely proffered his hand to guide his passengers carefully across the gangway. The couple then sauntered along the seven hundred yard long pier, one of the longest in Britain, which brought them eventually to the High Street and into the heart of the village.

Amy looked at her watch and told Jack they had half an hour or so before the Forest omnibus came, so they decided to take a stroll around the village. Jack pottered aimlessly while Amy busied herself with scouring the now increasingly depleted shops for a few items of food that she knew her mother would need. Forty-five minutes later they were safely on the bus as it trundled its way up and out of the village, through the tiny hamlet of Dibden Purlieu and onto the Forest heath. A dead straight roadway of nearly a mile brought them to their stop at a crossroads by a charming-looking public house bearing the name 'The King's Tavern', where they alighted and began the last two and a half miles or so on foot.

Autumn had faithfully painted the trees with its characteristic golds, reds and browns and Jack could sense Amy's simple delight at being in this place as they made their way along the narrow lane and deeper into the heart of the Forest. For quite some time they walked in silence enjoying the pure, clean air and the all-encompassing peace of the countryside.

Presently the odd cottage began to emerge here and there along the roadside, indicating they must be nearing Bucksleigh village. Suddenly, Jack spotted on their right, a grand, cream-coloured stately house looming up beyond the trees and a flurry of rhododendron bushes.

'Hey! That's not your house is it?' he asked, teasingly.

'Hardly!' said Amy. 'Country parsons cannot afford to live in such luxury, I'm afraid! That's the estate manor house. A number of the village dwellings were built for the estate workers at one time.'

Then, almost immediately on the opposite side of the road, Jack caught sight of the parish church.

'And this is your father's church then?' he surmised.

'Indeed it is. I've always loved this church,' Amy said. 'It has such a reassuring sense of peace and tranquillity and welcome about it. I come here on my own sometimes, just to sit and think; and to pray. I will take you inside sometime and show you.'

This spiritual guardian of the village was of warm, grey stone with hints of orange and, Jack had to admit, was a handsome, inviting-looking building. As they stood admiring it, the morning stillness was suddenly shattered as a happy chorus of excited children's voices rolled past them.

'What on earth is that I can hear?' asked Jack.

'Oh, that's the village school next door. Dear Mrs Tomkins and her little brood of youngsters! I used to attend the school when I was small. Mrs Tomkins was the teacher even then. I think she has taught there forever!'

They walked on and a short way beyond the village school the road turned sharply to the left while another narrow lane continued straight on between neat beech hedges and ancient oak trees.

Pretty cottages of locally-fired, yellow bricks with doorways draped in climbing rose bushes continued to straddle the road. And just around the bend which, Jack learned, was universally referred to by the locals simply as 'The Corner', the single village shop, no doubt in better times a veritable cornucopia of goods and wares catering for the needs of this rustic little community, stood untidily displaying its meagre offerings. A little way on was a tiny automobile garage, quite a rarity in such a backwater as this, which provided service for those wealthy enough to possess such a luxurious mode of transport.

Finally, some two hundred yards or so further, at the very far end of the village from the church, Amy steered Jack onto the crunching gravel driveway of the Rectory. It was a dull, rather sombre-looking building, again built from the local, yellowish brick and with high windows and a steeply gabled roof of brown slate.

Amy tugged excitedly on the bell pull and a few moments later the heavy oak door opened.

The Reverend Herbert Timmons was a portly, bumbling, jolly-looking man in his late fifties with a mop of wild, wispy white hair that struggled to cover his balding head.

'Hello, my dear!' he exclaimed, as his face lit up in a broad, wrinkled smile and his bright, sharp blue eyes twinkled. He embraced his daughter affectionately and then stood back to address her companion.

'And you must be Lieutenant Carpenter,' he said, taking Jack's proffered hand in both his own and beaming still with genuine warmth and interest in his guest. Jack at once warmed to this amiable man and his previous sense of unease evaporated immediately.

'Good morning, Sir. I am very pleased to make your acquaintance and it really is most kind of you to allow me to come and stay.'

'Nonsense my boy! We are only too pleased to have you here.

Amelia has told us much about you.

'Now, come on in, the pair of you. Amy, my dear, why don't you show Lieutenant Carpenter to the guest room while I call Mama from the garden and we can have a cup of tea together.'

Fifteen minutes later Jack and Amy were sitting in the homely front parlour of the Rectory. A large portrait of some dour clergyman hung above the huge oak fireplace, a couple of small watercolours graced the opposite wall and a variety of soft, dark brown armchairs and sofas along with an occasional table or two littered the room. In the corner stood a narrow, glass-fronted mahogany bookcase in which Jack noted a number of hefty tomes of theological works, sundry Bibles and hymn books. On a faded rug in front of the hearth, a ginger and white cat stretched and preened itself endlessly as only cats can do.

Presently the clink of china cups coming along the hallway heralded the arrival of the tea brought by Amy's mother. Jack stood immediately to be introduced and was greeted by a graceful and handsome woman of about fifty-five who smiled at him approvingly and without judgement. There could be no mistaking mother and daughter; Amy was an exact replica of Esther Timmons thirty years previously.

The tray was placed on one of the tables and when the rector appeared with a plate of digestive biscuits, cups of tea had been handed round and the formalities were over, Jack relaxed into the bosom of this open-hearted family who appeared like characters in a scene from some pastoral painting.

The conversation took a well-trodden route of discussion about the weather, the current privations of the duration, the progress of the war and the likely veracity of the latest reports leaking back from the Front. What Jack found refreshing and uplifting, however, was the heartfelt concern for others with which the Reverend and Mrs Timmons spoke, instead of the all too usual jingoistic nonsense that one heard so much these days.

Presently, Amy offered to take Jack outside to show him the extensive garden and the views across the fields towards the Solent, whilst her mother was occupied in the kitchen with preparing lunch and her father retreated once more to his study.

Lunch was a fine affair in light of the increasingly worrying food shortages. Lamb stew with dumplings and generous helpings of fresh carrots, potatoes and Brussels sprouts, all home grown in the garden. Jack indulged himself voraciously in such luxury, which tasted all the more delicious after weeks of somewhat bland institutional food in the hospital refectory and the monotonous rations of the Front before that.

During the afternoon Amy took Jack for a leisurely stroll around the village and its environs. He soon began to understand why she loved this place and the great Forest beyond. It was a sublime, quiet corner of all things English, a place so far removed from the chaos and madness of war.

They eventually retraced their steps to the church but this time they went in. The familiar mustiness of old stone buildings mingled with the sweet smell of timbers struck Jack straight away. They sat on the steps leading to the choir stalls and Amy chatted animatedly about the village and the history of the church. Jack listened attentively but also with pleasure at Amy's infectious enthusiasm in regaling him with her fascination for the place.

There was mention of the village as far back as the Doomsday Book and there was no doubt a settlement of some kind long before that. The villagers would have made their living from sheep farming, a couple of small salt pans nearby and more latterly the brickworks, producing the characteristic, creamy yellow colour of the houses, which Jack had noticed earlier as they entered the village. And some, of course, worked at the manor house at the top of the village.

A chapel dedicated to St Barnabas had existed from medieval times, and was most probably built and serviced by the monks from Beaulieu. Later it was demolished and replaced by the present church of the same name.

'You were right,' said Jack, presently. 'It is a beautifully quiet place; one can almost touch the feeling of peace here.'

They sat for some minutes in silence, drinking in the simple serenity of this house of worship. Jack had never considered himself to be particularly religious, yet he could not help but sense a calm, soothing presence of something infinitely benign and at the same time infinitely powerful in this quiet and unassuming little corner of the world. It seemed to transcend the horrors of the battlefield and the arrogant efforts of blustering generals and politicians to shape the times in which he lived.

That evening after supper Jack found himself alone with the Reverend Timmons as they sat together before a soporific log fire flickering in the hearth of the parlour, while Amy helped her mother with the dishes in the kitchen, in order to leave the men to talk.

'So, Lieutenant, Amy tells us you were wounded on the Somme,' the rector broke the silence.

'Yes, on the day the attack started actually. Things had hardly got going really. I cannot remember much about it to be honest. Apparently I was in Boulogne for a bit before being shipped back to Netley.

'Your daughter has been very kind to me, Sir. She is a wonderful nurse. I cannot thank her enough for all she has done to help me.' Jack hoped he wasn't blathering too much but he found the older man's gentle smile and kind, bright eyes reassuringly accepting and understanding.

'This whole war is a devilish business,' replied the clergyman, 'and what makes it worse, in my opinion, is the so-called patriotic nonsense which fills the newspapers these days. Please don't misunderstand me, Lieutenant. I have the greatest admiration for you brave young people answering the call of duty. But all this pointless loss of life – on both sides, may I say – makes me so angry. What will it achieve? Frankly, very little, I'll wager. Nevertheless, I have to say I am proud of my own two children for doing their bit: Amy with her nursing and our son Richard. I expect Amy told you that he's at sea?

'I just pray it will all end soon.'


Throughout the following days Amy continued to show the delights of the Forest to Jack. They visited Lyndhurst, the abbey ruins at Beaulieu, and even took the charabanc over to Lymington. They strolled along the shingle at nearby Lepe, gazing across the grey, cold waters of the Solent to the Isle of Wight. And as they stood watching the sea lapping tirelessly before them, every now and then they thought they could hear the faint, muted thud of the guns wafting across the Channel. Jack felt a shiver go through him; whether of the chilly air or of anxiety at the sound, he could not tell. As his hand brushed involuntarily against Amy's, his fingers instinctively and lightly folded around hers. Without a word spoken between them, she responded by clasping his hand more tightly and nestled closer to him, leaning her head upon his shoulder.

A thrill of happiness and contentment shot through his body and soul. Presently he turned to face her, looked deeply into her sparkling eyes and, casting aside his natural shyness, he kissed her inviting lips. She responded eagerly and with a passion and desire she had never before experienced.

\*

One afternoon as the dusk began to close in and Mrs Timmons had just brought a pot of tea and homemade scones into the parlour, they heard the front door close heavily and the Reverend Timmons very slowly and very deliberately make his way upstairs. Normally he would have popped his head round the door to greet one and all before quickly freshening up and then coming to join them. The look on his wife's face told Jack instantly that something must be amiss.

'Oh dear,' she sighed, 'I do hope everything is all right. He has been to see Mrs Betts. Both her husband and her son joined up you know.'

'What? Young Luke, Mama?' said Amy. 'But he can't be more than sixteen!'

'I know,' replied her mother. 'Apparently he lied about his age and got in. It is disgraceful that the army doesn't bother to check these things properly. Poor Mrs Betts. It's bad enough your husband going to war but not your only son as well. I do hope it's not bad news. Mr Nicholls called by this morning and asked if your father could drop in to see her.'

An hour later the Reverend Timmons appeared in the parlour, ashen-faced. It was also evident he had been weeping.

'I do apologise for not having joined you all for afternoon tea. Please do excuse me, Lieutenant,' he stumbled. 'It's just that I...I...I have received some shocking news; quite shocking.'

With an expression of utter despair on his face, the normally jovial clergyman slumped into his favourite, worn, brown leather chair in the bay window.

'When will this dreadful madness end?' he almost shouted with uncharacteristic anger in his voice and swept his hand through his mop of white, tousled hair.

'What is it, my dear?' encouraged his wife, lovingly, whilst Amy and Jack looked on anxiously.

'That poor, poor woman,' continued the rector. 'She is in a dreadful state. It's young Luke,' he sighed, his voice faltering.

Amy and her mother glanced at each other, wide-eyed in horror and for a while nobody spoke as the shock of the news sank in. Presently Mrs Timmons took the lead.

'What exactly happened, my dear?'

And the rector proceeded to relate the disturbing events he had just learned from the grieving mother.

Like others of his tender age, Luke had slipped into the army with ease, the recruiting sergeants only too willing to turn a blind eye to how old such boys actually were. And thus he had marched off exuberantly to the great adventure of war.

As fate would have it, he found himself drafted into the same battalion as his father to whom he had always been very close. When Henry Betts discovered what had happened, he was at first furious with his headstrong and wilful son, yet secretly proud. He even boasted to his pals about having his son fighting alongside him in the great crusade for the freedom of the civilised world.

But in the current firestorm raging at the Front, it seems that young Luke's bravado had finally run out. During a particularly vicious counter-attack by German forces in his sector, he had simply broken down in abject terror, hidden in a foxhole and curled up in a ball, sobbing. Two days later he had been discovered by a patrol out searching for the wounded. He was dragged, whimpering, before the C.O. and summarily charged with desertion and cowardice in the face of the enemy. It continued to be expedient for the army to ignore the fact he was under age and should not even have been there in the first place. The customary brusque court martial was held and the boy was sentenced to be executed by firing squad.

At dawn on 3rd December, Luke Betts was led out into the cobbled courtyard of what had once been a farm but was now a temporary barracks some two miles behind the lines.

The cold, early morning light slunk between the aged, stone buildings beneath a sullen sky. He was tied to a post facing a six man execution squad, as orders were barked out and echoed through the frosty air. Behind the line of his executioners stood four companies of soldiers, including those from Luke's own company, ordered to witness this macabre pantomime of justice.

The military authorities maintained it was essential for good discipline to stage such public executions. With little ado, a blindfold was tied round the sobbing boy's head as he tried in vain to beg for some sort of clemency.

The sergeant in charge of the firing squad read out the hackneyed script as to why the punishment was being carried out. He ordered the firing squad to raise their rifles. To aim. To fire.

A clamour of rooks, roosting in the nearby leafless trees cawed shrilly and fluttered up into the sky as the volley of shots split the early morning quiet. As blood fountained from his chest and abdomen, the boy's limp body slumped forward and down, as far as the ropes would allow.

At that same moment a chilling howl of anguish erupted

from one of the enforced onlookers, who then broke ranks and crumpled to the ground before his comrades, weeping uncontrollably. At the command 'Parade, dismiss!' Henry Betts was helped away by his companions.

As Herbert Timmons finished his story, his eyes began reddening once more with tears and a look of outrage clouded his usually cheerful countenance. Only the gentle, rhythmic ticking of the large mantelpiece clock and the occasional crackle from the log fire broke the stillness. Meanwhile, the shadows of the early winter evening began to creep through the tall window and fill the room with a darkness that matched the mood of its occupants.

As ever, it was Amy's mother who rose to the challenge of the situation, suggesting that they should spend a few moments in prayer for Mrs Betts; and for Henry, still isolated at the Front, unable to grieve properly and left to deal with the torment he had been forced so cruelly to endure.

Later that same evening a solitary figure made its way purposefully along the darkness of the village lane in order to bring comfort and solace to a desolate and grieving neighbour. It was Esther Timmons.

The dreadful episode cast a shadow across the entire village community and for not a few days Bucksleigh was a place touched by deep sorrow and mourning. Even the advent of the Christmas festivities did little to bring any cheer.

As 1916 rolled into 1917 a sense of the inevitability of further prolonged fighting enveloped all but the most foolishly optimistic. Rumours abounded, of course, of pending breakthroughs in the west, the hope of the mighty United States entering the conflict and the collapse of German morale. But Jack knew all this had been said before. He now had to face up to the fact that, as his wound healed, it would be time for him to return to the fray.

Amy had had to return to her duties at Netley and during the times she was away he had taken to making long walks through the Forest, revisiting some of the secret spots she had shown him but also discovering quiet places of his own.

One such place was a small clearing on the brow of a slight incline which looked out across the Solent towards the diamond shaped island across the water. Jack would sit for hours on the gnarled trunk of a fallen ancient oak, listening to the gentle sighing of the breeze through the trees behind him and the constant, reassuring washing of the waves on the pebbles below. Overhead, the familiar, intermittent cries of the seagulls echoed as they swirled and swooped along the water's edge in their endless scavenging for food. Jack loved the sound of the gulls; it filled him with a curious sense of nostalgia and a feeling of permanence, yet which he could not define.

Often he would also wander through the village and end up in St Barnabas' church, which was so special to Amy. There, he would sit quietly, sometimes for several hours, luxuriating in the solemn silence of the place. Shafts of winter sunlight played through the high windows and created small pockets of warmth where one could perch comfortably, alone with one's memories, thoughts, fears and aspirations.

Jack gave little thought to the concept of God in the traditional sense, although naturally he had attended Sunday school as a boy and observed the usual church festivals. And whilst a guest of the Timmons family, he had, of course, attended Sunday services in the church out of respect and because he recognised that it was important to Amy.

He thought about the Reverend Timmons, whom he had liked immediately from their first meeting and had since grown to admire greatly. He was a man of stubborn faith; an open, unpretentious soul who spoke the truth as he saw it and also without compromise, yet equally without judgement. He possessed a gentleness of spirit which offended no one. He was also blessed with a wry sense of humour. Jack smiled to himself as he recalled some of the anecdotes and jokes with which the rector had regaled him across the dinner table and the good-natured scolding he received from his devoted wife.

Jack revelled in being surrounded by the kindness and love of this deeply committed family and it was evident that Amy had been imbued with these qualities, which attracted him so much to her.

It was during one of these visits to the church on an unusually mild day in early January, that his thoughts began to turn irrevocably to the inevitable and his obligation to return to the war. As his mind wrestled with the terror of what this might bring, he heard the clank of the latch on the heavy oak door and turned to see the rector enter his church. When he caught sight of Jack, sitting in a sunlit corner near to the pulpit, he beamed broadly.

'Ah,' he began, 'a man after my own heart! I do like to slip in here sometimes, to pray and just to enjoy the peace and quiet. I find it helps me to think. To be in God's house is a good place to be when we need clarity and wisdom.'

'Yes,' replied Jack, 'it is a lovely spot and I know Amy loves to come here, too.'

'Amy has always loved coming here, ever since she was a child.'

'Sir, I want you to know how extremely grateful I am, both to you and your wife, for the extraordinary kindness you have shown me. Being here in the Forest and staying in your home have helped me hugely to recuperate. And, of course, being able to spend time with Amy. I am very fond of her, Sir, as I am sure you know. She is a marvellous person and you must be very proud of her.'

'Indeed we are. My wife and I feel most privileged to have been blessed with two such wonderful children.

'Of course you haven't met Richard yet, have you? Amy has no doubt told you all about him. He is a fine young man. I am certain you and he would get along famously. I hope you will have the opportunity to meet him one day.'

For some moments the two men sat in unforced silence, neither feeling any compulsion to make conversation but merely savouring the tranquillity which surrounded them.

After a while, the younger man spoke, 'Sir, may I ask how one is supposed to pray? I mean, does it work? Does God really listen to us?'

'Ah, the age-old question!' responded the rector. 'Well, before we can pray we need to believe that God exists! That's the tricky bit! But once we have crossed that threshold, then I find it helps a great deal to pray; particularly when things don't make any sense. And believe me, there is much that does not make sense in these present times. Oh, I must admit there are occasions when it seems as though my prayers are like empty words, which just bounce off the walls and the ceiling. But at other times I do catch a very real awareness of something or someone far greater than I, who is here and, as it were, is listening intently to me.

'The older I become, Jack, the more I realise how almighty the Almighty actually is! And how little I understand him. But I am consoled by the certain knowledge that he understands and knows me. And that is what gives me the confidence and the faith to believe in him and therefore to pray.'

'Thank you, Sir; that's helpful,' said Jack.

'Well, my boy, I had best leave you in peace. I need to drop in on Mrs Betts before lunch. I'll see you back at the Rectory.'

As the latch of the heavy door clicked into place, Jack looked up at the tall, arched window above the altar, through which the feeble warmth of the wintry sun crept its way in. And all at once he found himself verbalising the fears and hopes, which had been racing round and round in his head, into a kind of stumbling prayer.

He was not sure if the Almighty heard him but as he mumbled his muddled thoughts, he felt strangely peaceful.

# CATALYST

It was some days later that Jack suggested to Amy they might travel into town again. Thus, early one Saturday morning they caught the omnibus into Hythe and boarded the ferry to make the short crossing to Southampton. It was a surprisingly cheerful, cloudless day but with a biting chill that gnawed into the bones. Jack, however, felt impervious to such minor discomforts, for in his heart there rose an exhilaration that he could hardly contain.

After browsing through the shops they found themselves once more at the tea shop by the pier, where they had come on that first excursion from the hospital. It was busy when they arrived and they had to wait some minutes before a table became free.

As they settled to enjoy a cup of warming coffee and toasted buns, Jack could contain his excitement no more. Delving into his greatcoat pocket, he produced the little, silver-coloured box in which was the crocus-engraved locket he had bought at the jeweller's on their previous visit.

'Oh, you were going to give that to your mother, weren't you? It is beautiful,' said Amy.

'Well…actually,' he stammered, 'I…I really bought it for you. I've been waiting for the right time to give it to you. And I thought, well, today seems to be that right time! I do hope you will feel able to accept it.'

Amy was stunned. She blushed deeply and sat open-mouthed.

'But…but…'

'Please. Do say you will take it. I really want you to have it. I'm not very good at such things, Amy, but this is my way of telling you that I am very, very much in love with you.'

Amy leapt from her chair and threw her arms around him, sending a half-eaten toasted bun to the floor and coffee spilling onto the clean, white table cloth, much to the shock of the other customers and much to the horror of the elderly waitress.

'Jack, I love you, too. Very, very much indeed. And yes, of course I accept this. It's truly beautiful,' Amy exclaimed excitedly as she clutched the pretty locket tightly in her hand and looked admiringly at it.

It was now Jack's turn to cause a stir among the Saturday

morning coffee drinkers in the sedate tea room and to bemuse the waitress yet further. Standing up from the table he then knelt beside Amy's chair and took her hand.

'Amelia Timmons, would you do me the very great honour of becoming my wife?' he announced quite loudly and unashamedly, his face beaming as he did so.

Heads turned, eyebrows were raised and faces lit up around the room, as customers were treated to this scene of romance and chivalry. For a second or two there was a noticeable holding of breath by everyone present, in excited anticipation of the young lady's response.

Amy glanced around the room at the sea of smiling faces, whose war-weary, winter's day had been cheered by this little piece of romantic theatre.

She tilted her head to one side as she looked down at Jack's eager, grinning face and smiled that wonderful smile.

'Of course I will, Jack. You know I will!'

Spontaneous applause broke out in the tea shop and biddings of congratulations echoed across the room from all directions.

Later that day, as the afternoon shadows began to lengthen and the chill began to bite a bit more ferociously, the two lovers alighted from the omnibus at Hill Top crossroads to begin the two and a half miles walk back to the village, arm in arm. Amy's mind was tumbling with a million excited thoughts and her heart was fired with an exhilaration she had never before experienced.

'When shall we tell Mama and Papa?' she asked. 'And what about your mother, Jack? And when shall we get married? When do you have to return to you regiment? And then there's my job and Sister Truckett. Oh my, there are so many things we have to think about!'

He thrilled at her childlike excitement and felt a joy and contentment that permeated the very depths of his being. They stopped walking momentarily. Jack drew her closer to himself, wrapping his arms around her and hugging her tightly.

'You make me so happy, Amy. You are the most wonderful girl I know. I will love you forever.'

It was dark by the time they reached the Rectory and an icy rain was beginning to fall. Jack was grateful for the cosiness of the parlour with its thick, heavy curtains banishing the foul weather outside and for the hypnotic flickering of the flames, as they licked the logs crackling in the hearth. He sank into one of the deep, leather armchairs, immersed in his thoughts, while Amy had gone upstairs to change for dinner and Mrs Timmons busied herself in the kitchen.

It was as they sat around the meal table that Amy could contain her excitement no longer.

'Mama. Papa. Jack and I have something to tell you. We have decided to get married.' There. It was said.

'Well, rather, I should like to ask for the hand of your beautiful daughter, Reverend Timmons,' clarified Jack.

The rector looked up from his forkful of rabbit stew and grinned with a knowing look, his twinkling eyes shining with joy, while Mrs Timmons burst into tears of happiness, as is the prerogative of the mother of a bride-to-be.

'That would make us both very happy, I'm sure, Jack,' replied the clergyman. 'You have our blessing, of course.'

They all stood up from the table, Amy threw her arms around her mother and the rector offered his hand to his future son-in-law, 'Congratulations, my dear boy! I am absolutely delighted for you both. Such splendid news calls for a toast.' And he held up his glass of sherry and wished the two young people every happiness. Meanwhile his wife, still fighting back the tears streaming down her cheeks, embraced Jack warmly.

That night, as the rain clouds dispersed and went their way, a golden moon shone brightly over one very joyful household in Bucksleigh village.


The next few weeks saw a whirl of activity in and around the Rectory. Since Jack announced he was due to return to his regiment at the beginning of March there was no time to lose.

At Amy's request, her father was to marry the happy couple at St Barnabas' in the village and there would be a small reception held afterwards at the house. It was arranged for the banns to be duly read in the weeks leading up to the big day and Mrs Timmons worked her magic in her usual calm and unflappable way to have everything organised and prepared. Mrs Langley next door would arrange the flowers, Mr Goldman, the village shopkeeper would be only too pleased to procure a cake and dear Mrs Betts, God bless her, would help with the bride's dress.

Because of the short notice, the distances to be travelled and the vagaries of winter weather, not to mention the limitations imposed by war, not many family members would be able to attend. Amy's Aunt Harriet was going to be there, however, as she did not live too far away; and she suggested the young newlyweds might like to spend a few days at her cottage in Nether Wallop, a small hamlet to the north of the Forest in the direction of Salisbury and not far from the market town of Stockbridge.

'It's very lovely there,' enthused Amy, 'and it would mean we could have some time just to ourselves. I mean, without Mama and Papa being around all the time!'

'But what about your aunt?' countered Jack.

'Oh, she won't be there! A friend of hers' husband has been badly wounded and Aunt Harriet will be going straight up to Coventry to be with her for a while and to help when Jim comes home from hospital. Apparently the poor man has lost both his legs and Mary does not know how she is going to cope.

'Anyway, Aunt Harriet will be pleased to have someone look after the cottage while she's away. So you see, it all works out rather well!'

Jack chuckled at her enthusiasm for the plan and agreed it would be nice for them to enjoy a proper honeymoon.

'And what about your mother, Jack?' she asked for what seemed like the umpteenth time. 'I have not even met her yet.'

'She won't be able to come. It's a long way from Kent and she is not in good health. I have written to her,' he lied. 'She is very happy for us both and sends her love and congratulations.'

'Oh, I see,' said Amy, doubtfully, and wondered, not for the first time, why the man she loved seemed so reticent to share much about his family; or indeed, anything much of his past.

At last the happy day arrived. Miraculously, Richard was not at sea that month and had managed to obtain a forty-eight hour pass to attend his sister's wedding. Furthermore, in the absence of any friends or relatives of Jack in attendance, he had gallantly agreed to stand in as best man.

The weather was unusually kind for February on that day and the crocuses popped up their golden heads above the thin blanket of snow that covered the churchyard.

The service was an emotional affair as the Reverend Timmons not only 'gave Amy away' but also presided over the marriage of his beautiful, only daughter. Mrs Timmons wept in true style and there was much shaking of hands and were many affectionate embraces as the whole village turned out to wish the couple well.

The modest reception consisted of sausage rolls, luncheon meat sandwiches and, of course, Mr Goldman's delicious cake, all washed down with a glass of the rector's finest sherry.

And afterwards, Baines, the chauffeur from the manor house, with his master's blessing, drove the new husband and wife in style in his lordship's nearly new 1915 Alvis all the way to Southampton station. From there they were to take the train to Salisbury and hence to make their way to Nether Wallop and the longed-for seclusion of Aunt Harriet's cottage.

# THE COTTAGE

By the time they reached train journey's end, the light was fading fast and once more leaden clouds were building in the east, threatening to bring with them a blanket of snow during the night. The now Mr and Mrs Carpenter found a room for the night at the Wig and Quill, not far from the benevolent presence of Salisbury's magnificent cathedral.

After a welcome supper of cottage pie, cabbage and onions, accompanied by fine ale, they retired to their room, exhausted from the joyful busyness of the day, contented in each other's company and excited at the promise of pleasure in sharing each other's intimacy.

The following morning, after a hearty breakfast, the newlyweds made their way through the cobbled streets to St Thomas' church where, at Amy's behest, they attended the morning service and during which she silently gave thanks to God for the man standing next to her and for the happiness she felt, not merely in his presence, but also in his arms.

*The Cottage*

By late morning the threat of wintry showers that had lingered during the night had begun to retreat and so they ambled through the quaint streets and lanes of the city, savouring the quiet of a Sunday morning.

A late lunch at the Wig and Quill and they were ready to continue their journey to Nether Wallop. They lugged their cases to the broad market square where they managed to find a pony and trap that was heading for Stockbridge and which could drop them off en route. Huddled in the open landau with a thick, tartan rug against the cold, Amy felt elated by the prospect of a few days away from the arduous demands of the hospital, the pitiable sight of broken lives that streamed daily through its doors and the hawk-eyed surveillance of the fearsome Sister Truckett.

She took Jack's arm, snuggled against him and smiled as she watched his sharp, blue eyes taking in the gentle countryside rolling past, its stillness broken only by the regular clip-clop of the horse's hooves.

'A penny for your thoughts?' she asked presently.

'Oh. Sorry. What?'

'I was just wondering what you were thinking about? You're very quiet.'

'I was thinking what a very fortunate and happy man I am! If I had not been wounded, if I had not ended up at the hospital, if you hadn't been on duty that day and it hadn't been you who wheeled me in, I would not have fallen in love and married the most amazing girl in the world!'

And with that he hugged her even more tightly to himself and stroked her soft blonde hair.

'I do so adore you, Jack Carpenter,' she said.

'And I you, my darling Amy.'

Some fifty minutes later, the trap pulled over. Jack and Amy clambered down, and the driver helped them with their bags. Jack thanked him for his kindness and handed him two shillings. As the driver flicked the reins and the horse drew away, Amy, still holding Jack firmly by the arm, guided him into the lane which headed northwards off the main road and which ran parallel to a tiny rivulet that gurgled its way southwards.

A further fifteen minutes, and as the sun was slipping silently out of view, they reached Aunt Harriet's cottage.

Nether Wallop is one of those quintessentially English villages: a cluster of ancient, timber-framed cottages huddled along the banks of the Wallop Brook and brooded over by the squat, Saxon church perched on a small rise. Further on, the old manor house sits proudly atop the valley side.

Alongside its sister villages of Middle Wallop and Over Wallop, Nether Wallop is a tiny gem of tranquillity tucked away, nestling by a quiet tributary of the River Test which winds its way from the chalk plains east of Salisbury to lose itself in the mighty Southampton Water and where it meets its companion, the River Itchen.

Aunt Harriet's unpretentious little home lay on the outskirts of the village across the fields from the manor house on a single-track lane leading into the village.

Jack studied the dark-grey, slated roof and whitewashed walls punctuated by intricately leaded windows and the peeling, green front door, which was crying out for a much-needed coat of fresh paint.

'Wait here,' commanded Amy as she disappeared around the side of the cottage. A few moments later she reappeared, holding up a key in her left hand as though it were some sort of trophy.

Once inside and away from the plummeting temperature outside, they soon had a fire built in the large stone hearth and

Amy set to work in the tiny kitchen to see what she could find in order to prepare them a hot meal. Meanwhile, Jack hauled their luggage up the narrow, creaking stairs and into the larger of the two tiny bedrooms.

Some forty-five minutes later found the couple huddled in front of the fire and tucking in to a tasty vegetable stew, bread and dumplings, accompanied by a glass of Aunt Harriet's homemade elderberry wine.

'That was delicious, Amy. Thank you,' said Jack, as he carefully placed his empty plate on a nest of small tables and drained his glass.

'And I'm impressed with your aunt's wine,' he continued. 'A very noble vintage, I must say!' They both laughed and for a second, as their eyes met and the laughing subsided, a moment of sublime chemistry flashed between them.

Outside, in the blackness of the night, the wind moaned and whined its way around the cottage. But inside, the pair sat in silence for some time, she watching the flickering of the fire as the tongues of flame licked their way up into the chimney and he gazing at her, delighting in the loveliness of her sparkling, blue eyes, the tumble of blonde hair falling on her shoulders and the graceful sensuality that exuded from every part of her being.

'Amy,' he said softly, 'I do love you so very, very much.' For some moments she did not reply but continued to stare into the eager flames as they crackled and spat inside the hearth.

He felt momentarily desolate. Amy quietly moved over closer to him and taking his face in her soft, delicate hands kissed him long and fully on the mouth. He felt a rush of euphoria and desire course through his whole body. They fell into each other's arms and embraced with the passion of long-lost lovers.

The chilly morning light broke through the tiny leaded windows of the cottage to find the young lovers sprawled among a disorder of cushions and blankets in front of the dying embers of the fire.

It was Jack who woke first and, feeling the voluptuous softness of her naked body against his under the blankets, gently stroked her cheek and looked upon her with a feeling of complete contentment.

Presently he wriggled cautiously out from under the covers so as not to disturb her, pulled on his carelessly abandoned clothes and crept softly to the hearth in order to make the fire again. As the flames began at last to take hold, he padded into the kitchen and rummaged around to find what he needed to make some tea.

As he brought two steaming cups into the main room, Amy murmured and stretched herself awake. She looked up at him and smiled, gratefully taking the tea from him.

'It's going to be really cold today,' he said, glancing through the iced window. 'What would you like to do?'

'Let's take a walk into the village. I can show you the sights!' she teased. Jack laughed as he squatted in front of the fire to drink his tea and exult in the presence of this lovely creature.

Together with the other two Wallops, the curiously named little settlement's story weaves its way far back to ancient days and can claim to have borne witness to the endless changes of the tides of time.

Iron-age man first discovered that this quiet and sheltered valley amid the chalk downlands was an excellent place in which to make a home. Then people of a later age were similarly attracted to this idyllic corner of a green and pleasant land; these Saxon settlers built their church there to provide divine protection and spiritual succour for their farming community. And by the time another conqueror arrived, the village had clearly gained a status of significant importance to merit mention in King William's great survey of 1086.

Not far from the church Amy pointed out a rather imposing red-brick house where Aunt Harriet had once taken a part-time job as a chambermaid and where she had first met her erstwhile husband Horace.

Amy took great pleasure in recounting the much-loved, romantic and oft-told family anecdote of how they had first met. The story went that, whilst a young naval rating and home on leave, Horace had come to the village to visit his godmother who lived in one of the half-timbered, Tudor cottages built around the village square. Apparently, when he complained of having a severe headache, Horace's dear old godmother suggested he go along to the red-brick house, to see if they might have a suitable remedy. Ringing on the heavy doorbell, he was greeted by the attractive, young chambermaid, the sight of whom, so he always claimed, had a greater effect in curing his headache than the subsequent powder she administered in the scullery!

After walking out together for only six months, the young seaman and the pretty chambermaid were married at the village church of St Andrew and made their home at the stone cottage where the latest young marrieds were now billeted. Harriet and Horace were devoted to one another and it seemed that his frequent absence away at sea only served to deepen that devotion.

Sadly, however, they were never blessed with children, whom they would have loved and in 1912 the dedicated navy man, to whom Amy referred fondly as Uncle Horry, succumbed to tuberculosis and passed away at the age of fifty-five.

'That's a beautiful story; but also a very sad one,' said Jack.

'You would have loved Uncle Horry,' replied Amy. 'He was always such fun and made me laugh. And Aunt Harriet, as you know, is ever so sweet. I think she views Richard and me as the children she could never have. When we were younger and whenever they came to visit, she used to spoil us with lovely presents. I'm certain my parents thought it did us no good!'

Jack stopped, turned to look into her radiant, azure eyes and said, 'You are so absolutely lovely, I cannot see how it could possibly have done you no good!' And with that he took her in his arms and kissed her with an intensity that might have shocked any passing villagers.

They walked on hand in hand and Amy pointed out other places she thought might be of interest. Jack drank in the serenity of this tiny oasis of calm and normality, which made the war seem like some distant memory from a bygone age.

At the village shops they bought a few groceries to see them through the days ahead and as the sky darkened and snow clouds once more began to threaten, they scurried back to the cosy embrace of Aunt Harriet's cottage.

Thus they spent the following days, strolling hand in hand on grey, chilly mornings through the sheep fields and bare beech woods which surround the quiet hamlet, taking in the fresh, bracing air; sipping tea by the fire and talking and laughing on cosy afternoons; dreaming in each other's arms and making love through long, dark, late winter nights.

# THE PARTING

February wound its oft joyless way to a close with just the merest hint of a promise that spring was beginning to stir beneath the ground, readying itself to burst into life before too long. But now the young lovers' mood darkened, as thoughts turned to Jack's inevitable, impending departure, his return to his regiment and the dreadful uncertainty of what the future held in these troubled times.

As they strolled for one last time on a cold, dank afternoon across the rain- and dew-soaked meadows, down past Hatchetts Farm, and ambled through the village square and up to the church, Amy felt an increasing sense of foreboding. Had these past months merely been a dream? So much seemed to have happened and all so unexpectedly. Only last summer she was doing her bit at the hospital in the service of her king and country. And now here she was, married to this handsome, kind, shy but charming young officer, who had swept her off her feet. And these past few days in this tranquil spot had been some of the happiest of her life. Yet now, like some brutish and malevolent predator, this ghastly war was invading that happiness, as if to demand some cruel and undeserved retribution; to rob her of this beautiful man whom she loved with all her heart.

The thick, heavy wooden door of the deserted church creaked open on its ancient hinges as they entered and stepped softly across the timeless flagstones. Amy let go of Jack's hand and silently made her way up the aisle through the Saxon arch towards the altar. There she knelt reverently at the altar rail, fixing her gaze upon the stained glass window depicting Christ crucified. A flood of thoughts, hopes and fears gushed like a torrent through her mind and somewhere deep in her heart she prayed simply, as she had always done since a child, that whatever the future might hold, she might know God's grace to sustain her.

All at once she felt Jack's gentle hand as he caressed her hair and her shoulders and then knelt down beside her.

'I'm not much good at praying,' he said, 'but I remember something your father said to me a while back, that even though it's difficult perhaps really to understand God, he understands us and he knows us. And that made sense.'

'And it makes it easier, because he knows us,' Amy said. 'And I believe he also loves us and cares about us, too.'

The two of them remained kneeling in silence, both offering their own confused, silent prayers to the God who understood them; the God who knew them and loved them; the God who cared about them.

They walked back arm in arm to the welcome snug of the cottage, neither saying a word. The afternoon shadows began to fall at last as the light discreetly faded into the beckoning horizon to bring closure on yet another day. And with it, the thrill and excitement which had been Amy's during the past months, threatened to evaporate into nothing more than a memory.

Once back at the cottage, Jack fetched logs from the stack behind the house and built up the fire dwindling in the grate, while Amy busied herself in the kitchen to prepare their final meal together.

She had wanted it to be something special and despite the ever-growing shortages had managed to procure a small joint of lamb from the village butcher along with a few carrots and some winter greens from one of the farms. In Aunt Harriet's tiny larder she rummaged in a sack of potatoes and managed to find a handful of half-decent ones, which she proceeded to prepare together with the vegetables.

Later that evening Jack and Amy sat quietly, each deep in their own private thoughts as they tucked in gratefully to the splendid roast dinner which Amy had conjured up and washed it down with another bottle of Aunt Harriet's homemade wine. Dessert consisted of warm stewed apple sprinkled with raisins and thin, watery custard.

When the dishes had been done, the two lovers curled up together before the fire and gazed dreamily into its dancing flames, trying desperately not to think about tomorrow but to squeeze every last minute out of today.

Outside, the wind started to stir more earnestly and hum its haunting tune, as it found its path around the side and the back of the cottage.

'Please take care, my darling,' said Amy, finally breaking the silence. 'I love you so much, Jack, and I couldn't bear anything terrible to happen to you. It's not fair that you should have to go back. You've already done your bit; you've already been hurt. It shouldn't be allowed to happen again.'

'But I have to go, Amy. It would not be fair to the others if I didn't go. I will take good care, though, because I shall be constantly thinking of you. If it hadn't been for you, I don't think I would have survived my injury. In fact, I wouldn't have wanted to. You are the most wonderful thing in the world that's ever happened to me and I love you with all my heart.'

As the old brass clock on the mantelpiece, which had been a wedding present for Aunt Harriet and Uncle Horace, wearily chimed ten and the wind continued its tortured whine outside, Jack and Amy climbed the narrow, crooked stairs to the bedroom for the final time of their honeymoon. Fifteen minutes later they had nestled cosily under the thick blankets of the beech-framed bed and there spent their final moments of passion before drifting into a fitful sleep.

So it was that Jack now stood at the edge of the bed as Amy murmured softly, her eyes flickered open and she looked up and smiled as he gazed upon her.

'What time is it, my love?' she asked.

'Just before eight,' he replied. 'Mr Wheeler said he would pick us up at ten in order to get us to the railway station in good time.'

'Well, we don't have much to pack. And it won't take long to have breakfast and to tidy the cottage for Aunt Harriet.'

And indeed it did not. At ten o'clock sharp the pair stood waiting for old Mr Wheeler and his pony and trap to take them back to Salisbury. They had looked through the little house one last time to check they had not forgotten anything, locked the door and Amy had returned the key to its hiding place at the back for Aunt Harriet to retrieve.

A few minutes later and they heard the regular clip-clop of the horse's hooves, as Mr Wheeler came into view along the lane.

'Mornin', Miss. Mornin', Sir,' greeted the grizzled-bearded drayman in his broad Hampshire accent as he eased the trap to a halt. His sturdy, chestnut horse shook its head, stamped in the soft sprinkling of snow and snorted, sending a cloud of steam rising into the cold morning air as Mr Wheeler lowered himself from the wagon. He helped both Amy and Jack aboard before securing their two small, brown leather cases up front alongside himself.

The journey to Salisbury through the snow-laced countryside proved invigorating in the sharp, chill of the morning and the sun tried to be friendly, which helped to ease the anxious thoughts of the two young people. The amiable Mr Wheeler chattered merrily about this and that but Jack and Amy hardly heard him and simply muttered an occasional, polite acknowledgement to whatever it might have been that he was talking about.

As they entered the noble city, its ancient streets were already alive with the hustle of busy people going about their daily routines and the last traces of the snow had all but disappeared.

The trap turned into Fisherton Street and Jack fidgeted uncomfortably as the knots tightened in his stomach. When they finally pulled up outside the station entrance, he jumped down quickly and helped his wife carefully to the ground. Taking both the cases, he paid the drayman and thanked him for the ride. He then took Amy by the arm and, looking at each other with sad eyes, they made their way into the booking hall. Jack bought two tickets, a single to Southampton and a single to London Waterloo.

The latter train was due in little more than five minutes.

'Are you sure you have everything you need, my darling? Your papers from the hospital and everything?' Amy looked at him anxiously.

'Yes, yes. I checked them all this morning. Well, I don't actually have very much, do I?' smiled Jack, trying valiantly to appear cheerful. 'After all, when I arrived at Netley I only had the rags of my uniform! It was so kind of your parents to let me borrow some of Richard's clothes when I returned the hospital uniform.'

But his attempt at cheerful distraction had no success in fooling Amy. She looked up at him adoringly, her vibrant, blue eyes welling up with tears that rolled down her flushed cheeks. All at once she threw her arms around his neck and hugged him with an earnestness that seemed almost to border on desperation. He held her likewise tightly in his arms, stroking her soft blonde hair and fighting desperately to hold back his own tears.

They stood in their silent embrace, wishing in vain that time might stand still, and oblivious to the clamour of the station whirring around them.

Without pity, the shrill whistle announcing the arrival of the train to Waterloo invaded their momentarily private world and the chuntering, wheezing iron monster burst ruthlessly onto the scene, grinding and screeching to a halt, ending with a huge whoosh of steam. A dissonant clattering of doors and railwayman's shouts resounded along the platform as the train disgorged one throng of passengers and in its place swallowed another.

'Well, my darling, this is it,' said Jack as he slowly and reluctantly released her from his arms.

'Please be careful, Jack, and write to me when you can. I love you so very much. I always will, no matter what happens.'

'And I you,' he replied, with a brave attempt at a smile. 'Oh and please thank your parents again for their kindness. Take care, my darling. I love you, Amy.'

And with one final kiss he grabbed his case and stepped up into the carriage. The train was crowded with servicemen and civilians alike but he managed to find one empty seat next to the window. Hoisting his case onto the overhead luggage rack, he quickly pulled the worn leather strap to lower the window. Like so many others up and down the train, he leaned out as best he could to exchange those all-important, final few words of farewell with a loved one. He looked down and smiled again at his precious angel of mercy, who had rescued him from the abyss of complete insanity and restored to him not only a sense of normality but also a purpose and meaning to his existence.

'Dear Amy, please don't cry. I'll be home again before you know it,' he called, above the noisy din from the platform and the impatient hissing of the locomotive, trying desperately but unsuccessfully to sound optimistic.

With that, the trill of the guard's whistle pierced the air, followed by the ubiquitous shout of 'All aboard!', and another blast of steam signalled the grinding of the heavy wheels as they recommenced their endless turning toward journey's end.

Her eyes still wet with tears, Amy continued to wave as Jack's smiling face blurred into all the others still hanging from the windows amid the forest of waving arms, as the train clattered away growing steadily smaller and finally dropping from view beyond the intruding hills.

For some moments longer Amy remained rooted to the spot, staring into the distance, as if in a trance.

'Are you quite all right, Miss?' enquired a kindly voice. Amy turned, red-eyed, to face an elderly man dressed in his neatly pressed London and South Western Railway livery.

'Yes. Yes, thank you. Quite all right,' she lied and feigned a pretty smile.

Picking up her case she did her best to pull herself together and strode purposefully along the platform, crossing over the tracks via the red, wrought-iron footbridge and onto the opposite side in order to await the train to Southampton.

The locomotive belched and billowed its way into the station together with its caravan of reddish-brown carriages and Amy clambered aboard. Thankfully she found an unoccupied corner of the compartment where she could sit undisturbed with only her anxious thoughts for company and from where she could watch the wintry countryside as it rushed past the window.

'Dear Lord, please keep him safe,' she whispered and hoped that God was listening.

Within the hour the familiar sights and sounds of Southampton once more filled her senses as she made her way forlornly from the railway station through the busy streets and down to the ferry for the familiar trip across the harbour to Hythe. She was glad not to have to wait long and breathed in the salt spray air gratefully as the faithful old *Hotspur* sploshed its way across the water, which seemed more crowded than ever with the grey and camouflaged vessels of war, all playing their part in the struggle for victory.

Once at the other side, she took the omnibus up to Hill Top and from there wound her familiar way along the wooded lane to Bucksleigh.

As she turned into the driveway of the Rectory, the front door swung open and her mother all but ran out to greet her, throwing her welcoming arms around her and unapologetically weeping tears of joy to see her darling daughter once more.

'Oh, my darling Amy. How good to see you! Are you well? You look exhausted, my dear. Come on in and I'll make some tea. Now, how was your honeymoon at Aunt Harriet's? And how is Jack? When did he leave for London?' The barrage of questions continued, well-meant but unwanted.

After freshening up from the journey, Amy settled into the welcome comfort and sanctuary of the parlour, lounging in one of the brown armchairs, curling her feet up under her. Her mother brought in a tray of tea which she poured into pretty china cups decorated with an Indian tree motif and cut some neat slices of light Victoria sponge cake which Amy devoured appreciatively.

For quite some time mother and daughter sat in silence, interrupted only by the faithful, somehow comforting ticking of the old clock perched on the mantelpiece.

Outside the window the sky was anything but comforting as it glowered threateningly like a blanket of gloomy heaviness. Amy wondered where Jack might be at this point in time and what he might be doing. His explanation had been somewhat vague as to why he apparently needed to travel to London before reporting back to barracks in Chichester. Perhaps it was something to do with his having been wounded.

They sipped their tea and ate more cake.

Finally her mother spoke, 'Well, my dear, it is lovely to have you home again but I'm sure you must miss your dear Jack so terribly much. I am sorry he cannot be here with us, too. Oh, this dreadful war.'

'I know, Mama. But if it were not for this dreadful war, I would probably never have met Jack, would I?' Amy replied, trying to be positive.

'Well, that's true of course. And Jack is a fine young man and your father and I are so very pleased for you.'

'Where is Papa?'

'Visiting poor Mrs Betts again. That dear lady is suffering so from that dreadful business with young Luke, you know. Well, how could she not? Such a terrible, barbaric thing. And what with Henry still being away at the Front; the uncertainty of it all. I cannot imagine what that poor, wretched soul must be going through.'

'Yes, Mama. It all seems so unjust. The Betts have always been such a lovely family.'

'Anyway, my dear, how was your honeymoon? How were things in the village? I hope Aunt Harriet left you enough food in the cottage?'

'Yes, Mama. Everything was fine. We had a lovely time. Jack really enjoyed walking around the village and he thought the cottage was beautiful,' replied Amy, in order to satisfy her mother's endless curiosity, whilst all the time thinking of Jack. Where was he? How was he? Would she ever see him again? What if he were wounded once more? And even worse than last time? Such tortured thoughts spun round and round in her head while her mother embarked on relating all the latest news and gossip from the local community.

'Mama, if it's all the same to you, I think I should like to go and lie down for a while.'

'But yes, of course, my dear. I'll call you later for dinner and we can talk further. Papa should be back by then, too.'

# RETURN TO THE HOSPITAL

The following day Amy was to resume her duties at the hospital. After a quiet evening, talking with her parents and reading a letter from her brother which had arrived for them the previous day, she spent a restive night, waking every now and then, haunted by the constant worry for the man whom she loved so deeply.

She rose before the dawn, washed and dressed ready for the journey across the water and back to Netley and the stringent regime of the military code under the watchful, beady eye of Sister Truckett.

On her arrival she was met with a barrage of smiles and hails of good wishes from her colleagues. Even Brigadier Lightfoot, a crusty and irascible old orthopaedic surgeon, offered his congratulations. Her fellow nurses had taken a collection in her absence and presented her later that day with a very elegant silver-plated portrait frame.

'It's delightful!' exclaimed Amy. 'Thank you all so much.'

'We thought you could keep a picture of the dashing Jack in it while he's away,' ventured her friend Sylvia. And it was only then that it occurred to Amy, she had no photograph of him. Due to the whirlwind wedding they had not had time to organise a photographer so had planned to have some official pictures taken at a photography shop in Southampton when Jack was next home on leave.

In no time Amy was once again entrenched and absorbed in her work. The numbers of casualties arriving each day seemed never-ending. On a typically dull, damp March afternoon, a week or so after her return, yet another train rumbled into the railway halt behind the main edifice to deliver yet another cargo of hapless wounded.

On this occasion, however, harsh barks of command rang out above the usual, muted din of a transport, followed by the impatient clickety-clack of hob-nailed army boots hurrying up and down the narrow platform. Peering out through the broad, green doors of the main building, Amy could see armed soldiers drawn up in gauntlet fashion along the platform, as if forming a guard of honour for some dignitary or other.

More yells resounded along the platform, followed by the clatter of carriage doors as the train emptied its contents into the flurry of waiting orderlies and nurses. However, it was not some noble dignitary, nor the familiar tumble of bloodied khaki that Amy saw, but rather, a rag-tag band of some one hundred or so wounded German soldiers.

As they lurched and staggered or were helped along the platform and into the triage areas, Amy was struck by the looks of utter despair, uncertainty and terror on their faces.

Suddenly all the nationalistic propaganda and anti-German sentiment with which she, together with the rest of the populace, had been bombarded for the past two and a half years and which fermented in their minds, seemed to evaporate into the void of stupidity from whence it came. What Amy saw were broken, frightened human beings; some, little more than teenage boys.

'Get to it, Nurse! Don't stand there gawping!' crackled the voice of a senior orderly behind her, which startled her out of her momentary reverie and snapped her back into duty mode.

Efficiently and unfussed, she strode out onto the platform and made her way along the ragged line of forlorn prisoners as they straggled their way, or were wheeled or stretchered, into the bosom of the hospital.

As she reached the last but one carriage, an orderly called her over to help disembark a young lad of about eighteen. His field grey uniform was caked in yellowish mud and his right leg, or what remained of it, was swathed in a thick clump of dirty, blood-stained bandages. Training, professionalism and the objectivity that comes when one has witnessed so many horrific sights took over and Amy went about her business, easing the German into a wheelchair and steering him carefully towards the triage area.

Despite his evident pain, the young man said nothing and retained a certain dignity in spite of his distress and evident fear.

Amy studied his uniform for any indication of his rank but found no clue so guessed correctly that he was a conscripted private, called to take up arms in defence of the Kaiser and the Fatherland.

Desperately, she trawled through long-abandoned corridors of her memory to see if she might dredge up some odd words of comfort in German that lay there unused and until now, unneeded.

She recalled the middle-aged, motherly woman from Austria who had once visited the village many years ago and whom her parents had invited to stay with them at the Rectory.

Like any child, Amy had been amused by the curious way in which this lady had spoken and who had enthralled her by teaching her a few phrases of this alien tongue. For some weeks after Frau Kruger's departure, Amy had delighted in demonstrating to both her family and friends her newly-found skill to speak these strange words. Now she could demonstrate it more purposefully.

'Erm…*Ihr Name?*'

'*Mein Name ist Lutz. Manfred Lutz. Gefreiter,*' came the wary reply.

'Are you in much pain? Erm…*grosse Schmerzen?*'

'*Ja, aber klar!*'

'I am sorry, Private Lutz. Erm…*das tut mir Leid.*'

Even now a faint swell of pride at being able to put to use those long-buried words brought a flush to her cheeks. And to her patient, along with her infectious smile, they brought a hint of comfort into his present purgatory of suffering and fear.

A few days later Amy found herself in one of the 'German' wards. In order to guard against any possible escape, the wounded prisoners were housed in the main building of the hospital while the British and Commonwealth men overflowed into the ever-growing tented and hutted wards outside at the rear.

As she walked briskly along the lines of beds, a voice stuttered as she drew parallel with one of the soldiers. She glanced round instinctively and after a moment or two realised it came from the terrified young man she had accompanied through triage and into theatre just a week before. Amy smiled and went over to see what Private Lutz might want.

'*Schwester*...Nurse. How nice I see you again,' he grinned through crooked teeth.

'You are looking much better now, Private Lutz. I am truly sorry, though, that you have lost your leg. *Es tut mir Leid...* Erm...*das Bein.* But the doctors had no choice. You could have died... Erm...*sterben.*'

He grinned kindly at her valiant attempts to make him feel more at home.

'Yes, I know. Doctors are doing correct for me. I am not dying. Also I am fighting no more, too.'

Amy smiled at the quaint usage of the present continuous verb formations that so many foreigners seemed to struggle to apply appropriately in English.

'Would you like some tea? *Wollen Sie Tee?*' she continued, emboldened now by her growing command of German.

'Please, yes. *Danke.*'

She made her way past the armed guard at the end of the ward and reappeared five minutes later with the promised mug of hot tea. She sat with the young German while he sipped gratefully at this very English beverage.

'In England you has milk in tea; at home in Germany we have...er...lemon,' he observed, in an effort to make polite conversation with this humane and sympathetic soul.

'Where were you captured, Private Lutz?' enquired Amy innocently.

'I may not really say,' came the reply. But then, having glanced furtively around at his comrades, he whispered, 'At Aisne,' and grinned once more like a schoolboy, as though he were imparting some great, secret truth to someone who has no right to know.

'Which regiment do you belong to?' she pressed further.

'Ze twenty-eight Baden Division,' he answered with obvious pride, 'and... '

Their conversation was abruptly interrupted by a loud

commotion at the far end of the ward where an armed soldier was struggling to help two nurses contain a patient who evidently was hallucinating.

'*Schnell. Sie kommen, sie kommen!*' he screamed hysterically as he tried in desperation to shelter under his bed from the approaching foe that only he could see. His wide, frightened eyes glared at all around him and his face was contorted into a mask of hideous, abject terror.

Amy went over immediately to offer assistance and with a mixture of stern rebuke from the guard and a chorus of reassuring voices from the nurses, the demon of fear gradually departed from the man. He was helped back into his bed where he lay staring wide-eyed, breathless, exhausted. And utterly lost.


Four weeks after their parting on that anonymous and cheerless station platform, a letter arrived for Amy. She tore open the envelope with excitement as she recognised the spiked script.

*My dearest Amy,*

*I do hope this letter finds you well and that you do not miss me too much. I miss you terribly, my darling. My thoughts during the day-*

*time are always of you and in the night my dreams are filled with*
*your tender touch and your wonderful smile. You know that it wa.*
*that wonderful smile of yours that first entranced me! I think, too*
*of the carefree and happy days we spent at your aunt's cottage on*
*our honeymoon. I wish it did not have to end. It seems an age age*
*now. But I look forward longingly to the day we can be togethe.*
*once more.*

*Of course, I cannot tell you exactly where I am at present bu*
*things are not too bad here, apart from the dreadful rain there ha.*
*been. But I am quite well.*

*There is talk of yet another 'big push' being planned soon but w.*
*have heard this so often, I do not let it concern me too much.*

*My darling Amy, please keep me in your prayers and think of m.*
*often. I will write again when I am able.*

*Please give my kindest regards to your dear parents.*

*Your ever-loving husband,*

*Jack*

Amy read and re-read the letter several times, holding it to
her nose in the hope of catching even just a hint of his scen
and fingering it reverently in the comforting knowledge tha
his hands, too, had held this same piece of army-issue paper.

That night she prayed for Jack, as indeed she did most night and just as he had asked her to do.

The days passed quickly for Amy as casualties continued to flood unabated into the hospital. By now she had grown accustomed to witnessing the most horrific damage and injuries inflicted on human beings and no longer could any sight sicken her. Men with half their faces blown off, missing limbs, ripped torsos with their contents partially oozing out and figures blackened and blistered beyond recognition as living beings continued to be the daily reality of life and work at the hospital.

Was she becoming hardened and unfeeling toward this ocean of human carnage? Or was she simply executing her job in a professional manner? The truth is, she did not know.

One evening, whilst at the much needed retreat of home, when she had a few days' leave, Amy raised this gnawing problem with her father, confident that he would be able to bring his great wisdom to bear upon the subject.

Ever since she was a small child, she had held her father in awe as an endless source of knowledge, understanding and succour.

The clergyman listened calmly as his daughter poured out her heartache, her bafflement and her anger at the suffering which confronted her daily and her self-reproach at the apparent coolness with which she met it.

'Papa, why do all these utterly dreadful things happen? I have sat so many times in St Barnabas' and listened to you talk about a God who is good and who loves mankind. And I have always believed that. But right now I struggle to make sense of it. And what is worse, I don't seem to possess much pity any more.

'The casualties come in and I simply do what I have to do almost without thinking; and more and more, it seems, without feeling. Surely that cannot be right Papa.'

Her father nodded reassuringly and understandingly at the daughter on whom he doted.

'My dear, do not reproach yourself for what you are doing. You have taken on a difficult, yet vital task in this gargantuan struggle in which we find ourselves. And I know you fulfil your duties and responsibilities well. Dear Jack assured me of that!

'The fact that you care for these poor men efficiently and professionally is what is important to them. Your personal feelings and a sense of pity will not help them recover. It is precisely your dedication, your care and your skill as a nurse that will help them to mend and meet whatever challenges may await them in the future.

'As for God and human suffering. Ah, well, that is indeed an age-old question that many ask!

'Do you remember when you and Richard were youngsters? I came home one day and there was a huge kerfuffle going on in the house. You were sobbing; Richard was yelling and complaining bitterly; and your dear mother was exasperated!

'You and your brother had sneaked into old Mr Parker's orchard to scrump some apples – all with the best of intentions, I might add! Apparently you wanted to surprise dear Mama with some apples to make a blackberry and apple pie. Richard had then slipped as he was descending one of the trees and gashed his leg open on the rough bark. So there he was in the kitchen, howling, while Mama was trying to bandage the wound. And you were sobbing because you realised you should not have been in the orchard in the first place!

'Oh, what a to-do! We had to call Dr Ferguson out, I seem to recollect, since it was quite a deep gash in your brother's leg.'

A look of amusement stole over Amy's face as she recalled the incident.

'At the time, at your tender age,' her father continued, 'it seemed to you and your brother that the end of the world had

135

just arrived. But it made not the slightest jot of difference to
how much your father and your mother loved you both. And
still do.

'You see, I think it is rather like that with God. We can find
ourselves in all sorts of scrapes sometimes but it does not mean
he does not care for us or no longer loves us. Richard could
hardly have blamed me or his mother for injuring himself
whilst scrumping apples, could he? The fact is, we were there
to help him and look after him in his hour of need.'

Amy was forced to admire the simplicity of her father's words
and the unshakeable faith they portrayed, with which he
walked through life and which enabled him to make some
sense of it.

Thus, bolstered once more by her father's sanguine wisdom,
Amy returned to her duties with a renewed sense of purpose
and determination. She filled the long and often tiring days on
the hospital wards with new-found energy and compassion for
the hundreds of broken men who daily were carried through
the doors.

During the weeks that followed she received two further letters
from Jack which she would read and re-read for days after their

arrival with a mixture of tears of sadness, relief and joy. She would eagerly look forward to hearing from him again and, whenever she returned to Bucksleigh, the first question she asked her mother was whether there was a letter from Jack.

Yet, as the weeks stretched into a couple of months, and no more letters appeared, a sneaking sense of foreboding began to assail her thoughts.

At first Amy tried to dismiss it with every conceivable argument of reason and logic that she could conjure up; but in her heart, the pain and misgiving grew like some secret cancer. Daily she scoured the newspapers that were delivered to the hospital, to see if Jack's name might appear under the seemingly never-ending lists of casualties at the Front. She would repeat the exercise several times to convince herself that his name was not there. A short-lived wave of relief would sweep over her until the next day, when once more the bitter root of anxiety would start to spread its ugly tentacles through her heart and mind.

Rumours had been circulating for some time that another major push by the British was due and as Amy made her way along the corridors to her ward on the morning of 2nd August, she sensed a buzz of excitement in the air.

'Have you heard, Amy?' asked one of her colleagues.

'Heard what?' came the reply.

'There's been a huge push in Belgium, near the place the boys call Wipers. Apparently, they made significant gains in just hours,' her colleague continued excitedly. 'It's in all the papers!'

Amy hastened to the nurses' common room where, as usual, she found a copy of the morning's papers. She scanned the front pages which were full of the usual, exaggerated declarations of success, which fooled fewer and fewer people these days. The optimistic words of her colleague were echoed in all the papers.

A major offensive had indeed been launched just two days previously around a small village on the fringes of the British stronghold of Ypres. The pretty little town had already played host to two previous, bloody clashes and was where the insidious use of poison gas had, for the first time, been employed to such devilish effect. Now it seemed that yet again this once picturesque little town, or at least the skeletal ruins of it, must suffer still further devastation.

Amy wondered whether her dear Jack might be involved in this latest action and leafed through the pages to see if his regiment was mentioned. But before she could become too absorbed in the reports, she knew she must attend to her duties and had no wish to risk the rebuke of Sister Truckett. She made her way swiftly to her ward and set about her task of tending to the wounded and maimed, only too aware that within the following days and weeks, there would doubtless be yet another huge influx of casualties.

# PASSCHENDAELE

A blanket of thick, putrid smoke hung heavily over the flooded shell hole, which afforded only minimal protection in this pockmarked wilderness.

As dusk began to gather over yet another day's bitter and merciless combat, where the blood of 'civilised' men mingled with the mud and water of the ravaged and violated landscape, the figure in the hole shifted its position in a vain attempt to alleviate its discomfort.

His uniform caked in the infamous, yet now customary Flanders slime and drenched by the ceaseless and unforgiving downpours, Jack crawled cautiously to the rim of his foxhole. Despite the descending dark and smoke, he was only too aware that sharp-eyed snipers lurked still among the scorched tree stumps, the heaps of rubble that had once been peaceful farmsteads and the occasional rises in the otherwise shallow flat terrain.

A way off in the distance a chorus of heavy guns bellowed its incessant ode to death into the night sky, accompanied by the fire flashes spurting from the barrels of these iron behemoths of destruction. Next to him lay the mutilated head and torso of his companion. Together they had volunteered to scout the thin, still wooded ridge which ran to the left of their company and which, according to the major, might offer them some advantage in achieving their objective.

The two men had crawled, squirmed and crept their way inch by inch towards the ridge, stopping every now and then in the hope of avoiding detection or to wait patiently for another barrage of gunfire to pass over them and provide a short window of opportunity to make further painstaking progress.

As they reached the cover of the hole, a shell hit from nowhere, ripping his companion's body in half and smashing most of his head into a pulp. Jack vomited as he looked aghast at the horrific sight only feet from him.

Now he was alone. And this could be the right moment. It might be his only chance.

As he started to scramble up out of the hole, suddenly he stopped and pressed his body against the saturated earth, the filthy water still almost up to his waist. He hardly dared breathe. In between the rhythmic thudding of the guns, the

141

sound of voices drifted towards him on the evening air. He strained his ears in a desperate effort to catch what they might be saying; but more importantly, in which language. As the voices drew ever closer, he remained frozen to the edge of the shell hole.

# CONUNDRUM

As she made her way, on an afternoon clearly determined to show that summer was still fully in charge, in order to collect some fresh bandages from the stores, Amy noticed young Private Lutz sitting with others on the grass outside, watched over carefully by two armed guards. Manfred beamed and waved to her as she drew near and called something to her in German which she did not understand. But she went over to him to enquire as to how his recuperation was progressing.

'Don't let these Hun blighters annoy you, Miss,' growled one of the guards.

'It is perfectly all right, Corporal. I know this man already. I treated him when he first arrived. We have spoken before.

'So, *wie geht es Ihnen, Herr Lutz*?' she asked proudly in her best German.

'Zank you; I am feeling each day better now.

'Please, I have here to show you a photo of me and my…er…*Kameraden*. Please, look!' And with that he rummaged in the pocket of his jacket to produce a crumpled photograph depicting a group of young, relaxed soldiers, some sitting, others standing, gathered around a table outside a rustic tavern, presumably somewhere in northern France.

'You asked my regiment, *Schwester*. Here, you see us!' he said, excitedly.

Amy took the photograph politely and studied the picture with mild interest.

Suddenly she broke into a cold sweat. Her hands became clammy and she felt a griping knot in her stomach followed by a wave of nausea. She froze, transfixed for a moment. And then, struggling desperately to maintain some vestige of self-possession, she turned to Private Lutz.

'This man here. Who is he?' she asked and pointed to a figure towards the back of the group who was smiling genially.

'Him? *Ach*, I not sure. I know him but not his name. He not in my *Kompanie*. Why are you asking, *Schwester*?'

'Oh…erm…I just wondered. He looks a little like someone I know, that's all. It's strange, isn't it?'

She continued staring at the smiling German soldier in the picture, a maelstrom of confused and torrid thoughts whirring through her brain and bitter tears welling in her eyes.

'Please, *Schwester*. May I have ze photo?' She broke out from her trance and, pulling herself together, reluctantly, yet politely handed the picture back to its owner.

For a moment she gazed at the young Lutz as he wrapped the treasured photo meticulously in a tattered piece of paper and placed it carefully back in his pocket.

Amy could scarcely move. Eventually she bade her patient 'good day' and hurried off to try to make some sense of the traumatisation she had just encountered. As quickly as she dared, she made her way back inside and along the endless green corridors, desperate to find some corner of solitude where she could attempt to gather her thoughts and digest what had just happened.

As she raced along, oblivious to all around her and deaf to the sharp-tongued enquiry from Sister Truckett as to what she thought she was doing and where she thought she was going, a deluge of questions cascaded through her mind and overwhelmed the half-hearted answers, reasons and excuses with which she tried in vain to stop them.

Having reached the refuge of the tiny storeroom lined with shelves of neatly-folded, clean dressings, Amy could hold in her distress no longer. Almost falling against the shelves, the strength sapped from her, she slid slowly to the floor, weeping uncontrollably.

Following close behind, the stern figure of Sister Truckett appeared in the doorway, staring with incredulity at the sight which lay before her. She paused. Then, with a benevolence and compassion that seemed to contradict her usual strict and officious manner, she crouched quietly beside her protégée, placed a motherly arm around the poor, shaking girl as she shed her bitter tears, and whispered with a tenderness in her voice that few had ever witnessed.

'There, there, my dear. Take your time and then tell me what all this is about. I'm here to help you, my dear.'

The minutes ticked slowly by and the older woman waited patiently for the girl to cry her fill until there were no more tears left to cry.

Gradually and stutteringly, Amy regained her composure, choking back the last remnants of her sobbing and, with a soft white lace handkerchief from Sister Truckett, dabbed her red, anguished eyes.

'I'm sorry, Sister,' gulped Amy, 'I'm sorry. I…I…'

'Shush now, my dear,' soothed Sister Truckett. 'There is no need to apologise. Clearly something quite dreadful must have occurred for you to feel like this. It is most out of character.

'When you are ready, explain to me what has happened. And then let us see what we can do to sort it out.'

After several more minutes, Amy related the whole episode of young Private Lutz's photograph and the shock of seeing the young, smiling German infantryman in the background.

'But you see, Sister, it was… at least, it looked to be the absolute image of my husband, Jack, I mean…Lieutenant Carpenter.' And with that a fresh fountain of tears began to flow.

'But it cannot be, surely,' she wailed. 'Please tell me Sister that it isn't him! But…it does look just like him.'

Sister Truckett listened thoughtfully, hugged Amy a little more tightly, as if to instil some reassurance and said she was sure it could not possibly be the lieutenant, 'After all, he is in the *British* army. I am certain there must be a simple explanation. Who did Private Lutz say the man in the picture was?'

'He didn't know his name, he said. They were not in the same company apparently.'

'Well, photographs are not always very good. It is doubtless just a coincidence that this German soldier looks like your husband. Anyway where is Lieutenant Carpenter at the moment?'

'Well, I don't know exactly. He has written to me but was not allowed to say where he was. And I haven't actually heard from him for quite a while now.'

'Now, the next thing we are going to do is have a cup of tea and then I shall ask Private Lutz to show me the photograph. I'm certain you are worrying over nothing. Come along my dear, let's go to my office and have that tea.'

Forty minutes later Sister Truckett was standing at the foot of Private Lutz's bed studying intently the face in the picture. She had to admit to herself that there was an uncanny resemblance to the young lieutenant in question who had been in the hospital. There was something about the way he was smiling. She handed the photo back and made her way thoughtfully back to her office. There, she found Amy waiting slumped across the desk, her head on her arms, utterly drained and exhausted from her crying.

She looked up and stared questioningly as the door opened and Sister Truckett re-entered.

'I will be honest with you, Nurse Carpenter. There is a distinct similarity to the lieutenant but it is most probably pure coincidence. Yet I can see how it must have been a terrible shock for you!

'Now, let us see what we can do to try to sort this out. To begin with, you are going home, my dear, and taking three days' compassionate leave. When you return to duty on Thursday, we will do a little detective work together and see if we cannot solve this mystery.

'As I said, I'm sure it is simply a very unfortunate coincidence; but clearly, for your sake, we need to get to the bottom of it. Now go and get changed and off you go.

'And, Nurse Carpenter, do try not to be too anxious. I'm sure everything will become clear and it will turn out all right.'

With that Amy stood up and thanked Sister Truckett for her understanding and offer of help. The unexpected kindness she had experienced was a side to the 'Iron Sister' she had never encountered before and which, in itself, gave her a little comfort and fortitude in the midst of her despondency.


As the evening shadows spread their fingers into the parlour of the Rectory before the red summer sun, as it continued on its downward pathway, slipping silently below the horizon, Amy sat calmly in one of the cosy armchairs, bit by bit relating the events of the day to her mother and father. She had always been grateful for the open and loving relationship she had enjoyed with her parents and knew that, whatever the circumstances, they would always support her.

Well practised in their pastoral rôle, the middle-aged couple listened quietly and patiently, allowing their beloved daughter to tell her story, not jumping in with hasty words of vain comfort or trite advice.

When Amy had finished, a not uncomfortable silence descended on the room, broken only by the faithful ticking of the old mantelpiece clock. Amy picked up her cup from the tray of tea her mother had prepared and sipped thoughtfully, waiting patiently for whatever wise words her parents might choose to bring to bear on her predicament.

At length her father spoke, 'My dearest Amy, this has clearly been a dreadful, dreadful shock for you. Yet how kind of Sister Truckett to come to your assistance and to give you time to recover. What a gracious lady she must be! And the fact that she is going to help you try to unravel this mystery.

'And that is precisely what this is: a mystery. Not a pleasant one, I grant you. Life is full of perplexing mysteries, my dear, and we have to accept the fact that sometimes that is what they remain and that we will never manage to solve them. It can be the toughest trial of one's faith. Our solution is to leave it in the hands of the one who knows all things and can fathom all mysteries, trusting that in some, perhaps strange way, it is woven into the pathway of our lives and somehow serves a purpose which only he knows. We must leave this one, too, in his hands.'

And with that the three of them bowed their heads and prayed.

Despite the twin shadows of uncertainty and anxiety that hung like a constant backdrop to her every thought, Amy slept surprisingly well that night and in the morning woke feeling refreshed and unexpectedly rested.

As she drew back the curtains to greet the morning, a panorama of blazing sunshine in a cloudless sky helped to assuage the wounds of the previous day. She stood at the window looking out across the fields beyond the garden and the tops of the trees to the hazy outline of the Isle of Wight in the far distance. And just for a moment she felt immersed in a strange and inexplicable calmness together with a quiet confidence that seemed to buttress her mind against the morass of confused thoughts which had sought to assail her.

A tasty breakfast of thick porridge, followed by warm toast and honey from Mr Langton's hives at the top of the village lane awaited her as her mother brewed a fresh pot of tea.

'Papa has already had his breakfast and gone out,' her mother explained. 'We did not want to wake you but thought it best to let you sleep in for as long as needed.'

'Thank you, Mama,' said Amy. 'Actually, I slept very well. So where has Papa gone?'

'Oh, he's gone up to St Barnie's to work on some damp he has discovered getting into the south transept. You know your father and how much that place means to him. He takes his stewardship of it so diligently. And of course, with it being so hard to find tradesmen these days, he feels compelled to sort these things out himself.'

Amy smiled, knowing how devoted her loveable father was to his calling and absolutely everything that went with it.

Many were the times he would be called out late in the evening to some poor parishioner in distress and might spend the entire night listening patiently to their sorrowful tale; or hold vigil at some sick soul's bedside. And early next morning he would be at St Barnabas', mending something or making some improvement or other to the fabric of the place, then making further visits to members of his flock before finally chairing a parish council meeting in the evening.

She marvelled not only at his boundless energy but also at his boundless forbearance and imperturbable good nature.

After breakfast she helped her mother clear the table and tidy the parlour before stepping out into the warmth of this August day accompanied by the merest hint of a light breeze that whispered in the tops of the trees. She strolled purposefully through the village, making her way to St Barnabas'.

She turned the heavy iron door ring, listening for the familiar click' of the latch and gently pushed the huge, oakwood door, trying desperately to keep the inevitable creaking to a minimum.

Entering the quiet, pale-lit sanctuary of the church, she glanced around to see a solitary figure hunched in one of the pews close to the choir stalls and recognised at once the tousled white hair of her father as he bowed in prayer.

Amy slipped noiselessly into one of the pews at the back and waited quietly. She looked up as strands of sunlight probed the reds, blues and yellows of the stained glass windows and cast a kaleidoscope of rich, vibrant colours onto the ancient stone floor.

She loved this place. It was a treasure trove of memories from happy, carefree days of her childhood, growing up in this quiet corner of England. Quiet that is, until this terrible war had come, rising like some vile monster that had lain dormant in the bowels of the earth for so many long years, waiting only for an opportunity to unleash its venomous fury. And like some fire-breathing dragon it now reared its foul and hideous head, spewing death and destruction, hatred and rage, heartache and despair in every direction.

Presently she awoke from her cogitation to see her father standing over her.

'So, my dear, what brings you up to St Barnie's on this beautiful morning?'

'Mama said you had come here to do some repairs or something so I thought I might be able to help.'

'Ah, that is most thoughtful of you! Actually I was just praying for you again - that the Lord will give you grace to stay strong in the face of this present dilemma and that you will know peace of heart and mind.'

'You are very kind, Papa. Thank you. I am sure everything will sort itself out. In fact I was thinking, since Sister Trucket has given me a few days' leave from the hospital, I might take the train to Chichester tomorrow and visit Jack's regimental headquarters. Surely somebody there will be able to help me; at least, reassure me where Jack is and with whom…' Her voice trailed off as she began to wonder whether she was simply clutching at straws.

'If it would help to put your mind at rest, my dear, then why not? In fact, I will accompany you to Southampton in the morning. I was planning to pop over sometime anyway to see the curate at St Michael's. There's a few things I wanted to chat to him about.'


By nine thirty the following morning Amy and her father were to be found aboard the *Hotspur* paddling its way across the water, a journey to which they were so accustomed. As ever, the harbour was crammed with a host of naval as well as merchant vessels of all sizes and description.

Disembarking close to the pier, they made their way up the High Street as far as Holyrood. There, her father kissed his daughter goodbye and wished her success on her mission, before turning left into St Michael's Street to meet with his colleague at the church and leaving Amy to continue her journey to the station.

She was tempted to jump on the tram but decided that on such a pleasantly warm morning, the walk would do her good. It would give her time to gather her thoughts and plans for the remainder of the day and the task which lay ahead; a day when she hoped at least some of the knot of anxiety inside her might be unravelled; a day in which she longed for the agony of uncertainty to be relieved.

On reaching the station, she bought a return ticket to Chichester and wandered on to the near-deserted platform to await the ten fifty-five train. She glanced around at her travelling companions: a handful of servicemen, a couple of gentlemen in business suits and one other lady, like herself evidently travelling alone. Almost on time, and shrouded in billows of snorting steam and smoke, the train rumbled into the station and drew up alongside the platform with a squeal of brakes. As always, the usual chorus of doors being slammed open and shut, shrill whistles and shouts of 'All aboard' echoed along its length.

Without difficulty Amy found a seat in a compartment and settled down by the window. The only other occupants were a young couple with a small child. The man was in army uniform and the little boy of about three years old sat contentedly on his father's lap playing with a small, colourfully-painted, lead toy soldier.

In no time the train was hurtling through the south Hampshire countryside and Amy watched as the fields, farms and hamlets of the South Downs rushed past. Just the merest signs of the end of summer were beginning to appear dotted upon the landscape, as it began preparing to relinquish its crown to the beckoning months of autumn.

Amy churned her thoughts over and over. To whom should she ask to speak? What should she say? Will they think her stupid? What if they refuse or cannot give her the information she wants? And myriad further questions stampeded though her brain.

Having stopped only briefly at Portsmouth en route they arrived in Chichester and the train ground to a halt with its usual puffing and panting. Alighting from the carriage, Amy made her way through the booking hall and out onto the street where she searched for a taxi. Since she had no idea whereabouts the barracks were located, she had resolved to reach them by the quickest and most straightforward means possible. It proved to be a wise decision for the barracks lay a fair distance from the railway station and within just a minute or two she was safely on her way.

The taxi dropped her off outside the stern, forbidding, red-brick bastion of the barracks' exterior. Amy swallowed hard and stepped out determinedly towards the khaki-clad lance-corporal on guard duty at the gate to accomplish her mission.

Half an hour later and after several explanations and enquiries with several military personnel, she found herself sitting in a sterile, white-painted anteroom, its walls lined with colourful regimental insignia on neat wooden plaques and long dark-framed photographs of groups of uniformed men posing proudly for the camera.

Above the door through which she had been ushered by an officious yet courteous sergeant, a large clock rhythmically tick-tocked the minutes away. Finally the door opened and a tall, fair-haired officer of about forty entered the room introducing himself as Major Peterson.

'Please, come this way, Mrs Carpenter,' he said kindly and smiled pleasantly as he showed Amy into an adjacent room.

Inviting her to take a seat before his desk, he asked if she would care for some tea.

'Thank you, Major. That would be most agreeable.'

The major spoke to an orderly outside the room, before then

settling himself in front of the window behind his desk. Through the window Amy could make out a troop of men undergoing drill practice and could hear faintly the barking orders of the drill sergeant.

'Now, Mrs Carpenter, I believe you wish to enquire about your husband, Lieutenant Carpenter.'

'Yes, Major. I understand perfectly that you may not be at liberty to pass on any information regarding his posting and such like but it's just that I have received no word from him now for some months nor have I had any official notification, should he have been wounded or…' Her voice faltered with a slight quiver and she fought hard to compose herself and to maintain her sang-froid.

'You see, I am becoming increasingly anxious to know if he is safe and well,' she continued, 'so I thought that perhaps you might at least be able to give me some reassurance as to whether he is all right.'

Just then a gentle tap at the door signalled the arrival of the tea which the orderly placed carefully on the desk and then quietly retreated, closing the door softly behind him.

'Do you take milk and sugar, Mrs Carpenter?' asked the major, as he leaned forward in order to pour the rich, dark brew into fine, white china cups adorned with the regimental crest.

'Just a little milk, please. Thank you.'

The major handed Amy her cup.

'I'm glad we can still drink decent tea despite these tumultuous times,' he said and smiled again in a gallant effort to help put this poor, anxious young woman at ease.

Amy sipped her tea gratefully and hoped that her hands were not visibly shaking.

'Whilst you were waiting next door, Mrs Carpenter, I asked the adjutant to track down your husband's records and the latest details we have of any…er…casualties.'

Amy braced herself for whatever news was about to befall her.

Outside, the muffled shouts of the drill sergeant and the corresponding crunch of marching boots up and down the parade ground permeated the room as they sat quietly drinking their tea, awaiting the arrival of the said records. Major Peterson scrambled to find a point of discourse in an effort to ease the tension.

'Have you had to come far today, Mrs Carpenter?' he enquired.

'From the New Forest. My parents live in a small village there.

and I work as a nurse at the military hospital in Netley just across the water.'

'Oh,' replied the major, relieved to have found some common ground on which to pursue a conversation, 'I know the hospital quite well. I have had occasion to visit there a few times myself. It's a magnificent building, I must say and a marvellous place where our men can be treated. May I say, what an admirable job you nurses do there?'

'Well, we all must do our bit to serve however we can.'

A further eternal minute ticked by as they both made strenuous efforts to elongate the welcome distraction of the tea.

At last another tap on the door was followed by the entrance of a junior officer who saluted his superior, nodded to Amy with a brief 'Good afternoon, Miss' and placed a single sheet of paper on the desk in front of the major, before retiring discreetly.

Major Peterson furrowed his brow in evident puzzlement as he picked up the paper and studied its contents. He cleared his throat and ran a finger briefly round his collar as if to try to alleviate the slight hue of redness which was doing its best to infiltrate his countenance.

He cleared his throat once again.

'Mrs Carpenter, the information I have here states that the regiment holds no record of anyone of your husband's name and rank. We do not have, nor ever have had, it would seem a Lieutenant Jack Carpenter in the regiment. I'm very sorry.'

The pause which followed seemed to hold the whole of eternity in its grasp.

A look of absolute horror swept across Amy's face. Her eyes glistened and she shivered involuntarily as a bitter chill invaded her whole being. She felt sick and the colour seeped inexorably from her cheeks.

'But…but that cannot be right. It must be a mistake, surely My husband is in the Royal Sussex. I know he is. Major please, tell me this is a mistake.'

'I'm afraid it isn't. The only record of any 'Carpenter' we have is that of a Sergeant Guy Carpenter, and he died of wounds sustained in action on 20th January 1915. It's all clearly documented. I'm most terribly sorry, but there is really nothing more I can do to help you in this matter.'

The tension in the dull, functional room was palpable and mutual embarrassment screamed in the silence. A full minute passed without a word from either party.

Amy stared blankly at the major's desk, wringing her hands in her lap, feeling utterly desolate and without a clue as to what she should do or say.

The major shuffled papers diffidently on his desk in front of him, as inwardly his thoughts raced to find a way of escape from this awkward situation, whilst at the same time affording this poor woman some crumb of comfort and providing her, too, with a means of escape as painlessly as possible.

'Do you have transport, Mrs Carpenter? I realise you have taken a deal of trouble to come here today. Perhaps I could arrange for a driver to take you to the railway station?'

'Oh, er…thank you. That's very kind, Major. I really don't know what to say. I'm sorry to have wasted your time.'

Summoning every ounce of self-control she could amid the despair and confusion that gnawed away inside her, each vying for supremacy, Amy forced herself to preserve her poise and retain a dignified courtesy.

She stood, offered a quivering hand to the major and thanked him again for his time. He in turn, offered his apologies for her fruitless errand and muttered some words of sympathy and hope that she might solve the apparent mystery of her husband's whereabouts.

A chirpy, fresh-faced corporal who spoke with a Cockney accent drove her to the railway station, bidding her a good journey as he helped her alight from the Vauxhall staff car which his commanding officer had put at her disposal.

As Amy stood on the station platform waiting for the train to take her back to Southampton, back to the hospital, back to the Forest and back to... who knows what, a fine drizzle wafted through the air, replacing the earlier sunshine and served to add further gloom to the dark clouds of despondency which swirled and glowered malevolently around her soul.

# RETURN TO NOWHERE

L oved and encouraged by her ever-supportive parents, Amy spent her time away from the hospital resuming her desperate search. Letters to the War Office and *The Times*, seeking information or knowledge about Jack, brought neither hope nor consolation. It seemed that the man whom she had nursed and with whom she had fallen in love had simply disappeared. Or did not even exist.

Meanwhile life went on around her, capriciously it seemed to Amy. News of the progress of the war brought some cheer to the home fires which kept burning. Yet another major British offensive on the Western Front was launched in November followed by a strategic victory for the new-fangled 'tanks' at Cambrai. Then the following month saw the symbolically important capture of Jerusalem from the Turks which was announced with much fanfare and jubilation.

And with the United States now having entered the war, there was a rising swell of cautious optimism that, at long last, the tide might just be beginning to turn.

Amy threw herself into her work at Netley, going about her duties both diligently and efficiently, caring for the injured and dying men who daily arrived at the doors of the great hospital. No one would have guessed that the heart of this pretty and caring nurse, so trim in her smart, blue and white uniform and who exuded such a graceful tenderness, bringing comfort and succour to the suffering, was utterly broken.

When at home at the Rectory on her days off, she would go for long walks through the Forest, seeking out those secret favourite haunts where she had played as a child and which still held the magic and joy of happier times.

The mighty oaks and noble beeches of this ancient woodland, which had stood sentinel for so many centuries, once more shed their leaves like tears, just as they had done a thousand times before, as the advance guard of winter began to make its presence known.

Sometimes she would sit for hours in her much-loved St Barnie's, taking in the familiar, homely, musty aroma that is peculiar to so many old churches. She would seek out a place in one of the pews where the thin autumn sunlight would stream through the window above the altar and fall kindly, to provide, albeit fleetingly, a pool of brightness and warmth in which she could bathe. The quietude of the place, together with that warmth and light helped her to think: to think of the past twelve months which had turned her world upside down; to think of Jack and to wonder endlessly where he was; how he was; even who he was.

Christmas that year was not a merry one for Amy. In fact, she volunteered to work as many extra shifts as she could at the hospital, in an effort to obliterate any thoughts of previous Christmases; and thereby, to smother any memories of happiness which might dare to surface.

After earlier signs of hope, the advent of 1918 was marked by the seemingly inevitable and tiresomely familiar stalemate on the Front yet again. There was little movement, and the guarded optimism during those final weeks of the year just ended, risked faltering and even fading altogether.

Indeed, that optimism was eroded completely when, on 21st March, as the winter was being chased well away by the spring, the Germans launched a massive offensive that saw them break through the Allied lines and make significant advances once more into an already battered and beleaguered France.

The few sad miles of ground won so tragically, so bitterly, so bravely and at such enormous cost on the Somme two years before, were overrun within a matter of days by the lightning boots of the Kaiser's Stormtroopers. It left both the British and French High Command bewildered and caused alarm bells to chime loudly through the corridors of power in both London and Paris.

The Germans had been anxious to strike first and decisively before the overwhelming manpower and resources of the American entry into the conflict could be fully implemented. Boosted also by the some fifty divisions released from the Eastern Front after the collapse and surrender of Russia and the ensuing turmoil of revolution in the Tsar's empire, the Kaiser's right-hand man, General Ludendorff, clearly thought he had the advantage. And he was determined to exploit it to maximum effect.

Essentially it was the last and only card the Germans had left to play. A rising swell of misery at home, brought about by nearly four years of war, was now festering into an increasingly anarchic discontent, fuelled further by the goings-on in Russia. It meant that victory at all costs on the Western Front was the only option. And at the start, it appeared it might prove to be the ace in the pack. The speed of the German advance was truly staggering.

Throughout Britain, a tacit sense of uncertainty, nervousness, disillusionment and, at times, even a hint of despair could be felt in the air. Conversations about the war were tempered with moderation. The tone of the newspapers had long since become more cautious and the previous over-optimistic jingoism had dissipated behind the columns and columns of dead, injured and missing.

In the meantime the wards and tented 'city' behind the main hospital building at Netley were now teeming with an uninterrupted influx of casualties. But not only casualties of the fighting. For another, even more insidious, yet unseen foe had entered the fray. Having hitched a ride on the troop ships from America, it was now creeping into every corner of Europe and would ultimately engulf nearly every continent on the globe.

They called it Spanish 'flu, merely because the newspapers in neutral Spain were free to report it, and particularly when the king, Alfonso XIII became gravely ill, caught in its foul grasp. The combatant nations of Europe, however, attempted to play down its significance, so as not to demoralise the population or give the enemy a foothold for propaganda. It snatched the lives, not only of tens of thousands of people at home, but also ran amok through the trenches with equal impartiality. Some three hundred thousand Allied troops became infected, at least a tenth of whom never recovered, suffering a ghastly end coughing blood and sputum, as their lungs disintegrated within their pain-wracked bodies.

Amy found herself working sometimes as much as seventeen hours a day and often seven days a week, as the hospital struggled to cope with this two pronged inrush of patients.

The brief snatches of sleep she was able to steal, whenever the opportunity afforded it, were all too often ravaged by gruesome visions of the abysm of human suffering in which she was embroiled. In one respect it meant that her mind could be focused on something other than her own personal tragedy. Yet at the same time, the depths of misery she encountered rampaged mercilessly through her imagination, as she wondered constantly what might have become of Jack.

Just occasionally during these calamitous weeks and months, Amy succeeded in being granted a brief leave of absence and returned to the haven of the Forest she loved and the sanity of home.

The walk from the omnibus stop at Hill Top along the lane to the village, brought with it a flood of memories of better times, yet punctuated with the pain of loss and uncertainty. As always, she was greeted and consoled by the affection and tenderness of her stoical parents who, it seemed, possessed that rare gift to remain stubbornly imperturbable, no matter what hell might have been let loose around them.

It was more often than not the case, that her father spent increasingly many hours comforting his parishioners, not only for the loss of sons, husbands and fathers engaged in the fighting, but also now those who had lost loved ones to the 'flu pandemic and whose day had been turned into night and whose ordered world into disarray.

Amy listened with shock and sadness as her mother, on more than one occasion, reeled off names from the village and surrounding area, not only of those who had fallen in conflict - young men with whom Amy had been at school, fathers of young families in the village, local tradesmen with whom her parents had done business over the years, but also names of those who had fallen victim to the current contagion. It appeared that these twin serpents of death, like nothing before them, were utterly merciless in their demented crusade to satisfy an unquenchable appetite for human life.

In such moments of despair, as ever, she could often be found sitting alone in the hallowed sanctum of St Barnabas' at the top end of the village. At least here she was able to find, albeit briefly, respite from the cacophony and chaos of a world gone mad. Here she could find a place, in which to try to make some sense of it all, not only in her mind but also in her heart.

# THE END IN SIGHT

During the long months of summer the tide of war gradually did begin to turn inexorably in favour of Britain and France and their allies once again. The key turning point of the Battle of Amiens, later referred to by the Germans as their 'Black Day', was to herald the tolling of the Kaiser's Empire's death knell. Any previous confidence of a definitive victory entertained by the generals of the German Supreme Army Command was now being steadily and unstoppably eroded; and this not only from without, as the entry of America swelled the ranks of their enemy to overwhelming proportions, but also from within, as ever-increasing disquiet and dissent on the part of the German populace bubbled to boiling point.

Already by October, whispers of a German defeat began to smoulder on both sides of the line until finally, sanity and human reason recaptured their rightful place at the eleventh hour of the eleventh day of the eleventh month.

As the mighty German Empire, which had stood and strutted so proudly upon the mainland of Europe, crumbled and disintegrated into chaos and anarchy, across the tiny strip of water that is the English Channel, a collective and uncontainable euphoria broke out in every town and hamlet the length and breadth of the land. The streets of the capital erupted with spontaneous dancing and merriment, town halls were festooned with flags and bunting and normally quiet rural communities overflowed with a heady mixture of relief and joy.

The following Sunday saw St Barnabas' packed to the rafters as the villagers came to give thanks for their deliverance and an end to the bloodiest of conflicts, that was to become heralded as 'the war to end all wars'.

The Reverend Timmons led his flock in grateful prayers of thanksgiving and preached a sermon like none he had preached before. In it, he urged his listeners not to let their faith be shaken because of the adversity through which they and their loved ones had come, but rather to look forward with hope to the future on whose threshold they now stood. He reminded them, too, of the challenge facing them as their compatriots returned from the trenches in need of healing, reassurance and help to readjust to some sense of normality.

And finally, he reminded them of the words of Jesus concerning forgiveness, and sought to extinguish the understandable, simmering resentment and flickering flames of vengeance that burned in the hearts of many towards their erstwhile enemies.

For Amy, whilst she, too, felt a deep surge of relief pulse through her veins as the news came through, there was still much work to be done at Netley and she remained busier than ever. The final shot of this 'war to end all wars' may have been fired, but the tide of wounded men continued unabated to flood the hospital and all but overwhelm the staff.

And, of course, the 'flu pandemic continued to hunt down its victims wherever it could, since it still held most of the world in its lethal grip. It spread its tentacles like a latter-day Black Death into every home and institution it could find. Amy and her colleagues laboured tirelessly to stem this new onrush of suffering until, by the summer of the following year, the deadly virus began to recede and finally slunk away into the annals of history.

In its grim wake it had left ten times more dead than the whole of the war and nearly one quarter of a million people in Great Britain alone.

In a strange analogy, Amy was reminded that only a short distance along the shore from the great hospital, once sat King Canute, who in vain bade the sea to retreat, in order to prove to his sycophantic courtiers that he was in fact human! He could not hold back the sea and Amy and her colleagues felt at times that they could not hold back the sea of human misery coming ashore with every day that dawned.

As the new decade dawned, and with it the hope of a new era of peace, the full horror of the legacy of what became known as 'The Great War' could be assessed and the task of recovery from the conflict, as well as from the Spanish 'flu, could begin in earnest.

Sadly, the noble sentiments and high hopes of a 'country fit for heroes to live in' failed in large part to materialise. Despite a seismic shift in social attitudes and conventions, for many life continued to be the daily grind of back-breaking work, if one could find any, whether on factory floor or on the land and a constant struggle against the often cruel winds of fate.

By 1922 the number of patients at Netley had reduced considerably, as one by one they had recuperated from their injuries and returned home; or had succumbed to their wounds and were laid to rest in the quiet cemetery situated amidst the gently waving pines adjoining the hospital grounds.

As the frenetic demands of the hospital had therefore likewise subsided, Amy made the decision to resign her nursing post and return to the refuge of the Forest. She had played her part and had done her patriotic best for the nation in its time of need. She had also made her own personal sacrifice; for the mystery of her beloved Jack ate away at her heart constantly and the chasm of grief had never healed over.

On one of her days off she heard from a neighbour that Miss Perks, the new village schoolmistress, was looking for an assistant teacher to help her with the increasing number of children now attending the little school.

Without delay she sent a letter of application to Miss Perks and was delighted to receive an invitation to visit the school.

On a pleasant April afternoon the following week, Amy made her way to the top of the village to the yellow-brick school house which stood next to St Barnabas'.

As she walked up the short gravel path to the large red-painted entrance door, memories of the carefree days of her own time here as a child came streaming back. She recalled once more the seemingly ancient Mrs Tomkins, who arrived each day from Hythe on her equally ancient bicycle and always wore a blue, knitted shawl, come summer or winter. She was a firm, no-nonsense teacher but also a kind one who nurtured and encouraged her charges with genuine affection. Amy had always liked Mrs Tomkins.

Shortly after the end of the hostilities, and after what seemed like forever, this dear, aged lady had finally retired from Bucksleigh School and moved into a home for gentlefolk at Brockenhurst, in which to enjoy her twilight years.

The village community had given her a memorable send-off, so many of the residents had been taught by her and guided through their early years. Amy had helped her mother bake a special cake to take to the retirement party and her father had made a moving speech, in which he paid tribute to the much-revered schoolmistress as, 'an indispensable part of village life who would long be remembered as a towering icon of the community and to whom all owed an enormous debt of gratitude'.

Amy enjoyed a nodding acquaintance with the present incumbent, Miss Perks, a young woman in her early thirties who lived in Beaulieu. She had heard favourable reports about her from her father who, as a governor of the school, had been nstrumental in appointing the new mistress and made regular visits to the school in his rôle as village rector to speak to the children.

Amy rang the shiny brass bell which hung by the front door and waited. Presently it was opened by a small boy of about eight with a mop of ginger hair and whom Amy recognised as Billy Woodbridge, whose father had been severely wounded at Cambrai, leaving him now confined to a wheelchair. The family lived in one of the farm cottages just along the road to Lepe.

'Good afternoon, Miss. May I help you?' enquired the polite but rather sombre-faced lad.

'Hello, Billy. I have come to see Miss Perks. It's Miss Timmons,' she replied, thinking that her maiden name might register more readily with the youngster.

'Please come in, Miss. I will fetch Miss Perks.'

Amy stepped into the entrance hall and was immediately transported back in time, as her sense of smell was assailed by the unique aroma of wood polish and disinfectant which seems to pervade all schools.

Along one wall of the hallway hung jackets, cardigans and caps on small pegs and in the adjoining single classroom a chorus of shrill and enthusiastic voices chanted their seven times table. Amy smiled to herself as wave after wave of happy memories swept over her.

Billy retreated into the classroom and a few moments later Miss Perks appeared. The children were now silent and Amy could see through the open door that they were studiously copying from the blackboard.

'Ah! Good afternoon, Mrs Carpenter. Thank you so much for coming. It is nice to see you. Please, do come through to meet the children.'

As they stepped into the busy classroom, whose walls were covered with an array of colourful pictures, writings, charts and lists of all kinds, the pupils stood as one to greet their guest. Miss Perks' introduction of Amy was met with a courteous chorus of 'Good afternoon, Mrs Carpenter' and at a signal from their teacher, the young students sat down and continued with their copying.

Amy spent the following hour and a half sitting in on the remainder of the day's lessons, observing carefully. As the large brass-framed clock above the blackboard struck three, and at the instruction of their teacher, the children obediently packed away their things, then stood behind their desks to wish Miss

Perks and their guest a pleasant afternoon, before filing out into the sunny remains of the day, taking their belongings from the pegs with them.

Sitting in the small 'office' at the rear of the school building, Amy enjoyed a pleasant hour over a cup of tea, chatting with the prim schoolmistress about the responsibilities and expectations of the post advertised. She took an immediate liking to this straightforward and personable lady. At the end of what proved to be a rather informal interview and without any hesitation, Miss Perks offered the job there and then to a delighted Amy.

'The truth is, Mrs Carpenter, you are the only applicant but that notwithstanding, I genuinely believe you would be the ideal person for the post.'

Amy felt curiously elated as she walked back to the Rectory. The feeling of being valued and needed again and having something fresh on which to focus her thoughts and energy brought a modicum of balm to her aching heart.


So it came about that, at the beginning of the summer term, Amy launched into her second career. She woke each morning with a new-found purpose and could scarcely wait to start each new day at the school. She adored the work with the children, most of whom she already knew, of course, and shared their pleasure in seeing their progress and achievement.

Miss Perks and she hit it off right away and formed a firm bond of friendship. This friendship deepened yet further as, in the course of the ensuing months working together, they each discovered the other's story of loss and sadness.

In 1914 Edith Perks had been engaged to one Harold Bowman. At the outbreak of war, Harry had put his medical training on hold so as not to miss out on the adventure of a lifetime and, like so many of his peers, excitedly took up arms to march off to teach the Hun a lesson. After all, it would be all over by Christmas, they said, after which he could return to his studies and marry his sweetheart, Edith.

Harry enlisted in the Queen Victoria's Rifles and after only basic training found himself heading for France in November. Edith received regular letters and cards from her charming fiancé, telling her enthusiastically of the continued training he was undertaking and the growing sense of excitement he and his comrades felt as they longed to get to grips with the enemy.

In April the following year Harry's regiment was embroiled in what came to be known as the Second Battle of Ypres.

According to the initial meagre reports that trickled back home and which were later verified, Harry had been swallowed up in a strange, thick, yellow choking swirl of smog which had flowed menacingly from the German lines. It had overwhelmed him and his unit, as they advanced to take a forward enemy position on the outskirts of the strategic little Belgian town that would later come to symbolise so much about this gargantuan conflict.

It was the first time poison gas had been used on the battlefield. Sadly, it was by no means the last. During the following months, as the true horror of this vile weapon emerged, Edith's pain only deepened as her imagination tormented her with visions of the agonising suffering inflicted on the man she adored.

When Edith received the news, like so many others, her world imploded, as in an instant her worst fears were realised; future hopes and dreams were cruelly wrenched away and her life seemed drained of any meaning.

But Edith was a woman of considerable fortitude and determined to overcome this dreadful tragedy. At the time, she was working at a small private school on the northern outskirts of London and she threw herself into her job without restraint.

Despite the constant, corrosive anguish that ate through her heart on a daily basis, few would have guessed that anything amiss had befallen her.

As the dust of war gradually began to settle and its legacy of monumental changes to the modern world began to unfold, Edith decided to make a fresh start and attempt to rebuild her life from the ruins in which it still secretly lay. Through various contacts she learned that a situation as village schoolmistress in the depths of the New Forest had become available, for which she duly applied.

And thus, as the new decade dawned, Mrs Tomkins' successor was appointed. Edith was cordially welcomed into the life of the village and soon proved herself a respected and popular young woman.

Each day she would arrive at the school with a smile and set about the task she had taken on, with gusto and dedication. None of her protégés would ever have had any inkling of the pain that lay behind their schoolmistress's cheerful countenance. Yet each afternoon, when lessons were done, the pupils had run and skipped merrily on their way home, the smile would evaporate from Edith's face. She would often slip unnoticed into the church next door to sit and savour the soothing solitude of the old building, sometimes to pray but always to weep.

It was on one such occasion, that the Reverend Timmons happened into the church and found Edith sitting with head bowed and sobbing almost inconsolably. In his usual kindly manner, he discreetly made his presence known and sat quietly a few feet away, allowing her the time and space she needed, in which to express whatever pain or burden of grief she might be carrying.

Gradually Edith managed to compose herself and dry the tears. Her attempts to proffer some sort of mumbled apology were waved aside by the clergyman, who offered a listening ear, should she wish to talk.

For the first time, this redoubtable young lady confided in someone her story of loss and of pain and of anguish. The rector listened with genuine concern and when Edith had finished her outpouring of sorrow, he opened the well-worn Bible he had been carrying. He leafed his way to the 121st Psalm, which he read softly in the quiet of the spring afternoon. As he did so, the sun's rays found their way through the west window, just as they did every afternoon, and bathed the nave in their healing light.

Although she could not say why, Edith felt an indefinable quietude settle in her innermost self, as if some bird of peace had alighted on the branches of her soul, bringing with it the gift of solace. For the first time in six years, she slept soundly that night.

She requested that the rector keep the news to himself, since she did not wish to draw sympathy from the village folk and certainly did not want her pupils to know. For them, she wanted to remain resolute and a beacon of hope and strength for their future.

In early April 1924, Amy suggested to her friend and colleague that during the impending school holidays, the two of them might cross the water to Southampton to visit the shops and perhaps lunch out in town. Her mother's birthday was looming and she needed to find her a gift. So on a mild spring day a week or so later, the two women found themselves on the *Hotspur* from Hythe as it plied its well-worn route across the harbour.

They spent an agreeable couple of hours browsing the stores only now beginning to fill their shelves and to display windows with luxury goods, which during the war had become so scarce

Amy eventually found a small brooch which she knew instantly her mother would treasure. Paying the eight shillings and sixpence, she tucked her purchase safely in her bag and the two women sought somewhere to enjoy a light lunch.

Almost without thinking, Amy led the way down the High Street to the same little tea shop near the waterfront, where she and Jack had enjoyed toasted tea cakes and where he had proposed to her in what now seemed like another lifetime.

They ordered cheese and cress sandwiches, some fruit cake and a pot of tea. They looked out onto the busy harbour, watching the kaleidoscope of vessels coming and going in and out of the docks. Amid the dowdy and weary-looking freighters with tears of rust running down their tired paintwork that chugged past, Edith noted a much newer and freshly-painted ferry which, by contrast, seemed to glide effortlessly through the water. She pointed it out to Amy, who had a sudden and ridiculous brainwave.

'Edith!' she exclaimed. 'Seeing that ferry gives me an idea. Why don't we go to Belgium?'

Edith looked at her companion in complete puzzlement.

'Amy, what *do* you mean?' she asked.

'You and I. We could take the ferry to Belgium. You could

look for Harry's grave. You know you have always said you wonder where he was laid to rest. And I... well, I could perhaps try to find out something about Jack.

'The War Graves Commission is there. Surely there must be people who could help us. I read in the newspaper a few days ago that lots of people are now going all over France and Belgium to find their loved ones who were killed and to see where they are buried. Apparently they have created beautiful cemeteries for our fallen heroes. Edith why don't we go?'

The more she talked, the more enthusiastic Amy became at the prospect and the more firmly the idea rooted itself in her mind.

Edith sat quietly for a while, trying to digest what such a venture would entail and what it might achieve; whether in the end, it would bring any consolation or merely greater heartache.

Eventually she said, 'Let's think about it carefully first, Amy. We would need to plan it in the school holidays at any rate. And the cost might well be far more than we could afford. And where would we stay? How would we travel around particularly in a foreign country? Have you ever been overseas before?'

Amy had to confess she had not, but by now her initial enthusiasm had grown into ecstatic excitement.

'Please say you will come!' she insisted. 'We simply must do it, Edith!'

During the weeks following this conversation, Amy started fervently investigating the practicalities and logistics that would be involved in realising such a venture. She spoke at length with her father and mother, who cautioned her against setting herself unrealistic expectations of what she might discover. However, they also acknowledged that an undertaking of this nature might just help Amy on her personal journey of emotional healing concerning the perplexing mystery surrounding her darling Jack.

# PILGRIMAGE

On 4th August, ten days after school had closed for the long summer holidays and, coincidentally ten years to the day since the outbreak of the carnage which had robbed these two young women of the men they loved, Amy and Edith found themselves on the platform of Southampton station together with two bulky leather suitcases, awaiting the train to take them to London. An air of excitement, mingled with not a little apprehension, surrounded them, as the reality of what they had committed themselves to do began to dawn on them.

Eventually the train steamed and clanked its way into the station, easing to a halt with the familiar squeal of the wheels. A voice boomed along the platform informing passengers of the train's destination and exhorting them to climb aboard. A porter helped the two women with their cases and they found a compartment occupied by an elderly lady, who smiled genially as they entered, and a young man in a sharp suit, who spent the entire journey secluded behind a copy of *The Times*.

## Pilgrimage

The train clattered its rhythmic way to the capital, calling briefly at Winchester and Basingstoke. During the journey neither of the friends spoke much but preferred to sit quietly with their own individual thoughts, looking out of the window as they passed through the rich greens of the summer countryside.

Some two hours later the train pulled into the bustling, noisy railway metropolis that is Waterloo Station. Only at that point did the young man opposite emerge from behind his paper and gallantly offered to help the women with their luggage as they all disembarked onto the platform.

At Edith's suggestion they found a small café in the station concourse, where they gratefully sipped a cup of milky coffee before continuing their journey.

Since Amy had never before been to the capital, Edith now took the lead. Whilst working in Barnet, she had often come into the centre of the city and was quite used to negotiating the crowded, busy streets. They decided to take a cab to Victoria, to save them struggling with heavy cases on the underground train and by mid-afternoon they were trundling through the lush fields and orchards of Kent aboard the train to Dover.

They spent a comfortable night in a small boarding house in the town centre from which they could easily reach the port the following morning.

Excitement grew as the two young companions boarded the steamer, neither of them having been abroad before. They stood on the deck enjoying the thrill of the wind in their faces as at long last the ship steamed out of the shelter of Dover leaving behind its looming white cliffs, and began lumbering its way across the Channel.

Two hours later Amy and Edith were standing on foreign soil and stared in wonder at this strange, new world to which they had been transported. The alien sights, sounds and smells of the place filled their senses with curiosity and only served to add to a feeling of excited anticipation.

The women spent two days in Calais during which time they managed to acclimatise themselves to this foreign land and also to arrange their onward journey to Ypres just across the border in Belgium.

It proved to be a somewhat convoluted train journey via strange-sounding places such as Tourcoing and Kortrijk to Ypres itself; but it also helped to enhance the sense of great adventure.

## Pilgrimage

In the early afternoon of Saturday, 9th August they reached their destination. They made their way out of the newly-reconstructed station, and after an entertaining conversation with the station master, comprising his broken English, incomprehensible Flemish, interspersed with much pointing and gesticulation, Amy and Edith meandered the few hundred yards towards the town centre and into the main square.

They had read in the newspapers and seen photographs of the utter devastation wrought by the war and now they could see with their own eyes the reality of the destruction. The plucky people of Ypres had made a start to rebuild their city from the rubble. But it was a mammoth undertaking that would surely take yet many more years.

Edith had been given the name of a small guest house which was still functioning and lay just off the main Grote Markt. In no time at all, they found themselves in the somewhat weary-looking reception hall of the Kosthuis Goosens and being greeted by a very polite, friendly young man who spoke impeccable English.

Yes, they had rooms free for the nights the ladies required. And yes, they could reserve a table for the evening meal which would be served between six thirty and nine o'clock.

Their bedroom was simply furnished in whites and greens but comfortable and homely and looked out onto the sombre cobbled street below. Both women were exhausted after the long morning's travelling and agreed upon a much needed nap before setting off to explore more of the town, slowly being resurrected from the darkness of the four long years of death and depredation in the previous decade.

After a leisurely stroll around the Grote Markt in the late afternoon sunshine, Amy and Edith were served a simple meal of pork, potatoes and red cabbage at the Kosthuis Goosens before retiring for the night and to prepare themselves for the objective of their venture.

Whilst Edith slept surprisingly well that night, Amy found little sleep as a maelstrom of hopes, fears and questions bombarded her mind and wove itself into her thoughts and sporadic, momentary dreams.


A light breakfast of rolls, cakes and coffee was served in the tiny dining room at half past eight, after which the two English ladies embarked upon their quest.

To the staff of the guesthouse this was nothing new. For the past four or five years, a steady trickle of anxious, hopeful

English women had arrived in the town, as if on a personal crusade to find the last resting place, or at least some crumb of information, about a husband, fiancé, son or brother who had never returned home after the apocalypse. It was a tragic scene, yet one which had to be played out, if these poor souls were to find any comfort at all.

A short walk from the market square, in a small road just off the Elverdingestraat, Amy and Edith found a large, timbered building housing the Imperial War Graves Commission office, where they hoped desperately to glean some information about the fate of Jack and Harry; or at the very least about where they might lie.

A complaisant English gentleman of about sixty, with thinning hair and small round spectacles, greeted them courteously. He listened intently to their stories with the same patience and respect with which he had listened to a thousand similar stories these past few years. He then asked the two ladies to fill out a form with the details he required and suggested they might like to return in a couple of days, during which time his colleagues and he would look into the matter, to see if the Commission could provide any definite information.

Amy and Edith returned to the Grote Markt and managed to find a small café where they sat quietly over a strong coffee and looked out on the busy comings and goings of the townsfolk.

For the next two days the women explored more of this sad little town which had suffered so much. They followed the line of the ancient city wall which wrapped itself tightly around the settlement and browsed through the handful of shops that lined the Grote Markt.

They spent a quiet morning sitting in the remains of one of several churches that once graced the town and which one day would be fully restored to match identically their former glory. Few words passed between the two friends, as each waded through her own labyrinth of thoughts, stumbling repeatedly over myriad questions and fears, which sought to hinder any progress along a rational path to satisfy their quest.

Eventually, Edith questioned whether they had even done the right thing in coming to Ypres.

'I don't honestly know,' replied Amy, 'but in a peculiar way I feel somehow closer to Jack - wherever he may be.'

The following day Edith and Amy returned to the War Graves Commission office. Both had endured a restless night, sleep and neither could manage to eat much in the way of breakfast that morning, such was the knot of nerves in their stomachs. An inextricable mix of hope and dread simmered like some cruel brew within them both and ultimately, would demand to be drunk to the dregs.

They spoke once again with the kindly gentleman they had met previously.

'Ah! Yes, ladies. I do have some information for you. Please, come this way.'

He ushered them into a small side room and offered them a seat, before pulling up a chair for himself at a small wooden table, and shuffling a sheaf of papers in his hands.

'Yes, I do have some information concerning Corporal Harold Bowman.' And he glanced at each woman in turn to see who might respond to his announcement, then turned to Edith as her eyes widened and she swallowed hard.

'I can confirm what you had already been told, namely, that Corporal Bowman most likely died here on the outskirts of the town on 22nd April 1915 - and probably as a result of the use by German forces of chlorine gas. There was a large number of casualties in his unit that day because of the gas. But due to the heavy shelling that ensued, it would appear that, unfortunately, his body was never recovered. I am indeed very sorry.'

He gave Edith a few moments to absorb the news before continuing, 'It may be of a little comfort to know that there are plans afoot to construct a memorial here in Ypres on the Menenstraat to commemorate all those men who gave their lives here, but whose bodies have not been recovered. Corporal Bowman is one such man whose memory, along with others, will be preserved for successive generations.'

A trickle of tears wove its way slowly down Edith's cheeks as Amy embraced her friend. There was a long silence in the tiny room, broken only by the muffled sound of voices from the main office and the closing of a door somewhere.

Eventually Amy cleared her throat and asked the man if he had any news at all of Second Lieutenant Carpenter.

'Yes, I was just coming on to that. I'm very sorry, Miss, but I regret to tell you that we have no record of anyone of that name serving here during the conflict. His battalion was indeed active here at one point; but it would seem that your husband was not listed. I am truly sorry that we cannot help you further.'

It was now Edith's turn to support her friend, squeezing her hand as Amy stared blankly in front of her at the plain, whitewashed wall, wondering if this were all some sort of pernicious nightmare from which she desperately hoped she might wake up.

'May I offer you ladies a cup of tea or a cup of coffee?' asked the gentleman thoughtfully, breaking the cold silence of despair.

'Thank you. That would be very kind,' replied Edith.

A few moments later two cups of strong, hot coffee arrived and the elderly gent discreetly withdrew from the small room to leave the women on their own to process the news they had been given and to compose themselves.

It was as the two friends were leaving and thanking the man again for his help, that the most ludicrous notion entered Amy's head. Almost without thinking, she suddenly blurted out to the gentleman, 'How does one go about applying to the Commission? I do believe I should like to work here!'

Edith stared at her companion in disbelief at what she had just heard. And even Amy surprised herself by such an uncharacteristically spontaneous and random announcement.

The man looked at her in complete stupefaction, slowly removed his spectacles, then looked at her again, as if to focus better and to check that he had heard her correctly and understood what she had said. A thin smile spread slowly across his lips and his deep brown eyes twinkled.

'Well, Miss, I must say, you startle me a little; but what a wonderful thought! We are always keen to take on people who wish to give themselves to this enormous, yet thoroughly worthwhile task. If you think you are serious and determined in your offer, then I can certainly arrange an interview with our regional director.'

'Yes. I am serious. I really want to do something here and to help in some way, however small.' And as the words tumbled from her lips, a thrilling sense of excitement and feeling of pending fulfilment swept over Amy's whole being. She beamed broadly at both the commissioner and at Edith, who stood dumbstruck at her friend's declaration of intent.

It was later in the day, as the pair was sitting at a very modest restaurant eating cold ham and salad that Edith ventured to raise the subject once more.

'Are you sure this is what you really want, Amy?' she asked 'Where on earth did the idea come from, and so suddenly?'

'I don't know, Edith. Perhaps I am just being a silly, romantic fool but I felt a sudden compulsion that I simply have to do something really positive. I may never know the real truth about Jack. But in some strange way, I feel so strongly that I need to be here, in this place, where that awful grisly war happened. To do something to help so many poor, bereft souls like us and… I don't know, to bring some sort of dignity to all those thousands of brave men whom we lost.'

'But what about your parents? What will they think? And moving to live in a foreign country? And what about your position at the school? Have you really given this any thought at all?'

'No, I haven't. But I know it's what I want to do. It's what I need to do. Please try to understand, Edith! As for school, of course I will work any notice that might be required.'

At Amy's request, Edith agreed to prolong their stay another week, during which time, true to his word, the elderly commissioner hastily arranged an interview with his superior. The latter was equally delighted, that this earnest, educated young woman wanted to enrol in such a noble cause. The interview turned out to be less daunting and formal than Amy might have feared and Edith was on hand to give her friend and colleague the requisite reference. A few more formalities would have to be gone through over the coming weeks but all being well, Amy could take up a post in Ypres by the start of October.

Following their return to the Forest, the ensuing weeks seemed to Amy to pass in a blur. She felt an increasing exhilaration welling within her as the long summer days began their gentle yet inevitable drift towards autumn.

Her ever-supportive parents listened patiently and quietly as she related to them the events of Edith's and her trip to Belgium: her vivid descriptions of the battered little community of Ypres valiantly battling its way back from the near-dead, like some delicate flower trodden underfoot and struggling to force its way up from the earth and turn its crumpled petals once more toward the sunlight; the heartbreak of the news both she and Edith received; and also the unexpected and possibly headstrong decision to work for the War Graves Commission.

'My dear Amy,' began her father, with that familiar sparkle in his eyes, 'you know that Mama and I will always support you in whatever you feel you must do. We will of course miss you greatly, and so will the school, that's for sure. But this is indeed a noble task you have chosen and we are proud of you

You have our full blessing and we will pray that you find this path rewarding in every way.'

Amy knew her parents would support her but she was pleased nonetheless to hear them put it into words. Her mother smiled lovingly at her and then said, 'How exciting for you my dear! And just think, we might be able to travel there to visit you one day!' And with that, as was her custom at such moments, she pottered out into the kitchen to make some tea. And to shed a quiet tear.

Being the end of the academic year, Amy was not required to return to the school to work any period of notice. In fact, Sarah Betts, whose brother had been so cruelly robbed from her family, had eagerly taken up Amy's suggestion to apply for her previous position at the school and after a formal interview, was duly appointed to work alongside Edith.

# THE MISSION

As September drew to a close and the trees of the Forest clothed themselves increasingly in their rich autumn colours, Amy retraced her earlier journey to London, to Dover to Calais and thence to Ypres.

The Commission had found accommodation for her with a homely family in the Sint-Elisabethstraat, not far from the town square. Mijnheer Janssens and his wife, along with their two young children, put Amy at ease immediately and made her welcome in their modest home. It had been rebuilt only a couple of years before and like others, stood a lonely vigil among the many skeletal buildings as the enormous task of resurrecting the town continued street by street.

Amy was shown to a pleasant room on the second floor at the rear of the house which looked down onto a small courtyard, where the family kept their bicycles and an assortment of clutter.

As she unpacked her things, an unexpected twinge of panic

bore its way into her stomach. Was she doing the right thing? Had she embarked on some fool's errand? Would it prove to be a disastrous mistake?

As she turned such questions over and over in her mind, her gaze fell upon a small embroidered plaque which hung on the wall opposite the window. It caught her attention because for some strange reason it was in English. It read simply: *Whatsoever thy hand findeth to do, do it with all thy might; for there is no work, nor device, nor knowledge, nor wisdom in the grave, whither thou goest.'*

Amy at once recalled the words from the book of Ecclesiastes and as she contemplated them, a fresh wave of confidence and determination flowed over her and she felt even more convinced that she was in the right place and at the right time.

The following morning she made her way across what was increasingly recognisable and navigable as a town to the Commission building. There she was greeted cordially by Mr Dunning, the kindly gentleman whom she had first met back in the summer and under whose guidance she would be working. Having first exchanged the usual pleasantries, Mr Dunning gave Amy a tour of the offices and introduced her to her new colleagues.

Her job brief was to help catalogue the names of the many thousands of men listed as 'missing in action'. In addition, she was to assist family members visiting the Commission, seeking the final resting place of their loved ones in one or other of the many war grave cemeteries so carefully and beautifully laid out throughout what had been referred to as the 'Ypres Salient'; a place now synonymous with unimaginable horror and a place where so many young men's lives had been so brutally cut short.

Despite the inevitable sadness of the task, Amy found the work enormously rewarding, especially being able to help others like herself, who desperately wanted information about a missing fiancé, husband or son. She could readily empathise with the despair and suffering she encountered and in some strange way it helped her, just for a while, to bridge the chasm of loss which still lay raw and gaping and open in her heart.

Thus for the next two and a half years, Amy buried herself in this humanitarian work and with it came a sort of healing to her own soul.

Occasionally the Commission would receive visits from its German counterpart, the *Volksbund Deutsche Kriegsgräber-fürsorge*, known simply as the *VDK*, which either sought infor-nation for one of its own or which was able to supply information on missing or killed British or Commonwealth personnel.

It was on one such occasion, a bleak, rather drizzly day in late February 1927 that a small, neatly-dressed woman in her mid-sixties appeared in the Commission offices. She spoke briefly with Mr Dunning who presently showed her into the small side room where Amy and Edith had once sat in vain expectation of hearing good news. He asked Amy if she would be good enough to assist this German lady, a Frau Zimmermann, who had been referred to them by the *VDK*.

Amy hurriedly scoured her memory for any scraps of German vocabulary and phrases that she might still be able to exhume from what she had learned all those years ago during Frau Kruger's visit and with which to offer her help.

'*Guten Morgen Frau Zimmermann. Mein Name ist Amelia Carpenter. Wie kann ich Ihnen helfen?*' she said.

The woman sitting opposite her smiled good-naturedly and took Amy completely by surprise, replying in perfect English, 'Thank you, Mrs Carpenter. But please, do feel free to speak English! You see, I originally come from England.'

'Oh, I see...but I understand you are here to enquire about a member of the German military.'

'That is correct. Please allow me to explain.' And with tha
she related her remarkable story.

# HANNAH'S STORY

Sigmaringen is a small, seemingly insignificant town which perches comfortably on the banks of the upper Danube, deep in the heart of southern Germany. A formidable-looking castle built on a stark, rocky outcrop on a bend in the river, stands guard over the cluster of buildings which makes up this sleepy, rural community.

As always on a Tuesday, Frau Zimmermann made her way to the twice-weekly market in the main square beneath the castle, to buy bread and vegetables and hopefully some eggs. She might even be lucky enough to procure some ham, although things were getting bad these days as more and more items became rationed or indeed, disappeared altogether.

Hannah Zimmermann had been widowed now for some twenty years or so. She had first met her husband on a chance encounter, when he had visited England in the late 1880s.

She had been working as a governess to the children of a Royal Navy captain at the family's rather grand Georgian house just outside the town of Tunbridge Wells in Kent.

On a typically overcast and blustery day in October of 1887 the captain had brought home to dinner two officers from the Imperial German Navy, whose ship was on a goodwill visit and had put into Chatham on its tour of sundry European ports.

The moment Hannah had set eyes on the winsome, rather shy, young German sub-lieutenant, she had fallen head over heels in love. His soft green eyes, neat blond hair and rather noble bearing awakened Hannah's youthful dreams of her ideal man.

The romance was a whirlwind affair. Despite some initial misgivings on the part of her parents, but with the blessing of her erstwhile employer, the couple was married within six months and Hannah went to live with her handsome new husband in his home town of Sigmaringen.

Located as it is, far inland, many miles from the sea and with the demands of Emil's naval career, life for Hannah was not straightforward. To begin with she had to learn the language. But she was a quick learner and with the help of dear Frau Bachmann, who lived next door, Hannah made rapid progress. Within three years or so, she could pass as a native speaker having shaken off entirely any trace of an accent and having developed that rare skill of assimilating authentic intonation.

Hannah and Emil loved each other deeply. His frequent enforced absences at sea meant they saw each other only intermittently but their devotion to one another grew only stronger.

The months stretched into years but before long a child was born, a son. In memory of Emil's father they named him Jens. He was a beautiful child and made his parents' happiness complete.

But then, when Jens was barely three years old, the family's joyous existence was shattered forever.

Hannah had just returned with the boy from their weekly expedition to the market, when the telegram messenger arrived with an urgent communiqué, postmarked 'Kiel'. As Hannah gingerly opened the envelope and unfolded the navy-headed paper, the unwanted reality of the horror of its contents began to bore its way into her brain.

*'It is with deepest regret that I have to inform you…'* The sentences dissolved into a blurred mess of cruel words before Hannah's eyes, as their meaning twisted like a hot knife into her heart.

Apparently it had happened all too quickly and no one could

have foreseen or prevented such a tragedy. During manoeuvres in the Baltic Sea, it seemed there had been some sort of accident aboard Emil's ship, which resulted in a small explosion, killing both Emil and another junior officer.

Hannah sat for some while staring blankly through the kitchen window which gave directly onto the slow meandering river. And while little Jens played innocently at her feet, the tears streamed down her cheeks as she sobbed with unutterable grief for the only man she had ever loved.

Thus it was that Hannah Zimmermann became a young widowed mother. After much agonising soul-searching, she made the brave decision to remain in Germany. Having lived there now for six years, she felt it her home. She was content with the rural existence and felt in some way she owed it to her soul mate Emil to live out her days in the land to which he had brought her as his bride. Her friends and neighbours were good to her and she would be able to visit Emil's grave in the cemetery frequently, which she did. And besides, if she returned to England, there might be problems in receiving the small naval pension to which she was now entitled.

Despite doing so alone, Hannah made a fine job of bringing up young Jens and won the admiration both of Emil's relatives and her neighbours. She took a part-time administrative job working at the town hall to supplement her meagre income but devoted her spare time to making Jens' life happy and complete. At home she made a point of speaking English with him so that by the time he was eight or nine he could converse confidently and with ease in either his mother's native tongue or that of his homeland.

It happened on this particular Tuesday in the autumn of 1916, as Hannah was returning from her trip to the market that she bumped into old Herr Baier, a former teacher at the town's secondary school who had taught young Jens for several years. He enquired concernedly after the boy, knowing that news had come recently that he had been presumed missing in action, somewhere on the Western Front. Hannah shook her head sorrowfully and the genteel Herr Baier touched her lightly on the arm in a vain attempt to reassure her.

'There is much confusion there at the moment, Frau Zimmermann. Many of our boys are missing. But every day, you hear of more turning up safe and sound. Jens is a resourceful lad and a good soldier. I feel certain he is all right. Take heart, my dear!'

'Thank you for your kindness, Herr Baier. Yes, I am sure you are right,' replied Hannah, doubtfully. And as she turned away to continue her journey home, it was all she could do to choke back the tears welling up from within.

As the days stretched into weeks, Hannah filled the long empty hours with busyness in an effort to keep her mind occupied and to suppress the festering heartache of a broken spirit. But each evening she would light a dim candle and sit by the window which looked out onto the ceaseless, ever-rolling Danube and trace her fingers over the grainy photographs of her beloved Emil and her precious, precious Jens.

Round and round in her mind would revolve the interminable questions as to how life could be so capricious and why she should be punished in this way.

And each morning, as the postman delivered the mail, she would hurry excitedly to the letter box outside by the front door in the hope that there might be some reassuring news or at least some snippet of information on to which she could hold and which might bring even a modicum of comfort and cheer.

Then about three months later she heard from old Herr Baier that one of Jens' comrades had returned home to the town to convalesce, having been wounded at the Front and hospitalised in Frankfurt.

Hannah immediately made arrangements to visit young Albrecht at his parents' home in the Antonstrasse, one of the town's main thoroughfares.

He and Jens had been in the same class at school and had joined up together when the war started.

Hannah hoped against hope that the young man might have news of her darling boy. Having lost the only man she had ever loved, she could not bear the thought of losing her only child as well.

It was a cold morning that day as Hannah made her way nervously to her appointment. Her heart was beating fast and all manner of wild imaginations raced through her head, anticipating what news the young soldier might be able to bring her: yes, Jens was wounded, too, but he was all right and they will release him from hospital soon; he's been captured by the enemy but they treat their prisoners well; he became lost in the battle for a few days, but soon made his way back to the lines and he's fine; probably the telegrams have been held up somewhere. And so on.

Hannah hesitated before knocking tentatively at number 21.

A moment later the door was opened by a sombre-looking woman of about her own age, dressed in a drab, black dress, her hair tightly pulled back in a bun and a look of much pain etched into her face.

'Frau Zimmermann, do come in. This is most kind of you to come and visit Albrecht, especially as… well, since the news of your dear Jens.'

'Thank you, Frau Krämer. It is good of you to let me come. But the boys were… I mean *are* such good friends and I was wondering whether Albrecht might know something… anything at all about Jens' whereabouts.'

A faint look of horror mingled with pity cast itself like a shadow across the other woman's face and she said only, 'Yes, well, do come through to the sitting room. Albrecht is resting.'

As they entered the rather dark, oak-beamed room with its clutter of heavy furniture and thick maroon curtains at the window, Hannah gasped silently at the sunken, sallow figure sitting on the sofa. He looked like some lost, bewildered child and his vacant eyes seemed to be gazing at some far distant object.

The young man did not move. He was oblivious even to their presence in the room and continued only to stare interminably nto another world.

'Albrecht, dear. Frau Zimmermann, Jens' mother, has come to visit you. Is that not very kind of her?'

With excruciating slowness, the boy turned his shaven head to fix his gaze upon the source of the voice and then at his visitor. Hannah did her best to return his vacant stare with a friendly smile but struggled to conceal her horror, as the realisation of the boy's condition struck her.

She had read in the newspapers of soldiers suffering from what was termed shell shock. All at once a deluge of pity overwhelmed her, as she recalled young Albrecht and Jens running, laughing and shouting excitedly as they played together as youngsters on the banks of the river.

'Please do sit down, Frau Zimmermann. Would you like a cup of coffee?' continued the boy's mother cheerily, in a valiant yet rather sad effort to carry on as though all was well and perfectly normal.

'Thank you. Yes. Yes, a cup of coffee would be very welcome.' And as Frau Krämer softly retreated into the kitchen and busied herself with the coffee, Hannah smiled once more at Albrecht whilst her mind raced to try to think of something to say to alleviate her shock and hopefully to engage the boy in conversation.

'So, Albrecht, I expect you are glad to be home and able to enjoy your mother's excellent cooking again. It must beat army rations any day! Her cakes especially have a fine reputation in the town!'

Her opening gambit was met with silence.

'Albrecht, you do remember Jens, don't you? Are you able to tell me how he is or where he might be? You were together at the Front, I believe. It's just that, well, apparently he is missing and…'

At this point Hannah could not stop the tears from flowing freely down her cheeks. In the same instant Frau Krämer returned with a tray of coffee which she set down quickly and hurried to comfort Hannah with a tender and sympathetic embrace.

'There, there, my dear. I'm sure Jens is all right. Try to be brave. This wretched war is taking its dreadful toll on us all. But we must stand firm and be strong.

'Albrecht, my dear, can you tell Frau Zimmermann anything about Jens? Did you see him before you left the Front?' she pleaded, hopefully. But the boy merely continued his indifferent, empty gaze and remained imprisoned in his own shattered world.

Hannah battled to pull herself together and regain some composure and apologised for her lack of self-control. But Frau Krämer would hear none of it and did her best to convince this poor woman that all would surely be well.

They drank their coffee and made small talk for half an hour or so before Hannah took her leave, thanking Frau Krämer for allowing her to come and for her hospitality.

She trudged sombrely back home as dark clouds began to gather threateningly above and served only to reinforce an ever-increasing shadow of gloom and despair that hung over her.

The following months saw Hannah busying herself yet further in a vain endeavour to distract her mind from the ever-fading hope of ever seeing her precious son again and to keep at bay the terror of receiving the ultimate grievous news that she feared.

Then, on a drizzly day in late September, as the last throes of summer were fading into a chilly, rain-soaked autumn, the news she had been dreading for so long finally arrived. As she caught sight of the blue-uniformed telegram boy pause outside the front of the house, lean his bicycle against the clean, white fence and walk slowly up the path to the front door, Hannah braced herself with every whit of courage she could muster.

After what seemed an eternity, a timid knock came at the door. Hannah wiped her eyes with the long, embroidered apron that she always wore around the house and moved briskly now to face the terror which haunted her daily. She thanked the fresh-faced, young lad courteously and as he retreated discreetly back down the path, she let the door swing gently to a close as she stared hypnotically at the dull, grey envelope in her quivering hand.

The simple communiqué delivered in cruelly matter-of-fact terms, the conclusion that, due to no further information concerning the whereabouts of her son, he must, regrettably, be presumed dead.

Hannah read and re-read the message a dozen times, her eyes glistening, and transfixed each time on the word 'dead'.

In a numbed stupor she walked slowly back into the living room, laid the telegram upon the dresser and picked up the photo of Jens in his new army uniform, grinning with youthful exuberance at the great adventure that lay before him. Her fingers gently traced the outline of his face as her tears dropped onto the glass. And then, with a howl of pain that can come only from a mother bereft of her young, she slumped into a chair and sobbed bitterly until there were, quite simply, no more tears to be shed.

For three days Hannah neither slept nor ate nor left the house.

Finally she found the strength of will to venture out once again into the town. She pulled on a thick, brown woollen coat and studied her gaunt face in the tall gold-framed mirror, which hung lugubriously in the hallway, straightened her lifeless, unkempt hair and pulled on a maroon, felt hat against the impending cold and wet outside.

This time she made her way to the cemetery and to the grave of her dear Emil. The sky was heavy and full of cloud and the rain drizzled steadily and without pity. She tramped solemnly through half-deserted streets, where people scurried for shelter and cast curious glances at the lonely figure that seemed oblivious to the foul weather, trekking relentlessly to her destination.

As she reached the cemetery and knelt on the ground beside her husband's headstone, the rain seemed to beat down even more heartlessly, sploshing on the ground as if in some kind of cruel show of triumph.

'My dearest, dearest Emil,' Hannah said, as she caressed the top of the shiny, black marble stone engraved in gold letters with the name of her husband, 'we have lost our darling boy. I am so sorry. And they don't even know where he is or what happened to him. But he's gone. I pray only that God will guard his soul and give him rest.

'I am so, so very sorry, Emil.'

Hannah remained at the graveside for some time, as the cold rain continued its monotonous rhythm and the sky grew ever darker.

At last she stood up and, drenched through and with her tears mingling with the drops of rain streaming down her cheeks, wove her weary path back through the empty, friendless streets to the lonely refuge of her home.

So it was that Hannah Zimmermann, now alone in the world, lived her days in quiet solitude. Despite the goodwill and good intentions of her neighbours and friends to help ease her pain and lift the heavy burden of loss, she sank further and further into an abyss of melancholy.

The war wound its wearisome and wasteful path for yet a fur

her twelve long months until finally the stalemate was breached. The newspapers were suddenly filled with alarming and often contradictory reports of what exactly was happening at the Front. Unrest festered in the streets and taverns; rumours of defeat and pointing fingers of blame spread like a cancer through the populace until, at last, the slaughter and folly ground to a halt. Then chaos and confusion broke loose across the country. Young men returned home feeling bitter, betrayed and disillusioned; politicians argued and ranted as to who was at fault and what path this broken nation should now be allowed to follow, while ordinary citizens worried only about finding enough food to put on the table for the next meagre meal.

Towards the end of September, 1926, as Hannah once again made her regular visit to the market, she noticed a young man standing on the corner of Fidelisstrasse, handing out some leaflets. From the tattered military greatcoat he was wearing, Hannah surmised he must be a former soldier, perhaps seeking work or charity in these depressing times.

She took one of his leaflets and there read with interest about the growing work of the *VDK*. The article also mentioned the offer of assistance to the bereaved to visit the graves of their loved ones as well as to trace missing or lost relatives from the war. A mix of grief, excitement and curiosity began to stir within Hannah and almost at once she felt compelled to pursue this offer of help. To what end she was not sure. But it had to be done.

On her return home she pulled some paper from the small beechwood bureau in the living room and set about writing to the address given on the leaflet to request help.

It was some five weeks later, and almost as she had given up hope, when a small, brown envelope with an official-looking postmark was dropped into the letter box. Eagerly, Hannah slit open the envelope and pulled out its contents. There was a polite reply to her request and another form to be completed requiring further information about the person she wished to trace. That same afternoon Hannah filled out the necessary details on the form and posted it back.

A curious kind of hope crept into her heart and lifted her spirits as she went to bed that night.

Thus, early the following year, Hannah Zimmermann was sitting on the train heading northwards towards the Belgian border. It proved to be a long and tiring journey with some five changes of train and an overnight stop in Aachen as well as a somewhat protracted wait at the border while the necessary paperwork was checked and re-checked. But none of this mattered to Hannah. If it meant she could discover something, anything, concerning the fate of her only son, then it was worth a journey to the ends of the earth.

When the last train of her quest finally pulled in to Ypres late on that February afternoon, the sun was already beginning to fade in deference to evening's approach.

The small guesthouse which the *VDK* had helped to arrange, was a short walk from the station and Hannah was grateful, at long last, to find some respite from the previous two days' travelling.

Although courteous and civil, the landlady of the guesthouse clearly viewed German visitors with an air of contempt and some suspicion. Presumably she was only willing to accept such guests because it helped to augment her otherwise sparse income. However, Hannah was too preoccupied with her personal mission, than to be concerned by the understandable prejudice of her hostess.

After a welcome and much-needed night's rest, she made her way the following morning to the *VDK* office, which lay somewhat hidden away on the outskirts of the town in a place called Langemark. And there she spoke with a Herr Kraus who had, in preparation for her visit, made some initial investigations.

Jens' regiment was at Ypres during the battle in 1917 and had also been in France at the now infamous Battle of the Somme the previous year. Although his name was listed in accounts of various actions undertaken by his unit, it appeared to have been inexplicably omitted on a couple of occasions, which was most out of the ordinary. Furthermore, and despite the official notification that Hannah had received all those years before, the *VDK* had no reference of his having been killed, wounded, taken prisoner or missing in action.

Following some further scanning of various documents, each one raising Hannah's hopes only for them then to be ruthlessly dashed, Herr Kraus concluded with much regret and deepest sympathy, that he could not in fact trace Jens' whereabouts or what might have happened to him.

He tried his best to offer some fragment of comfort in explaining that there still remained confusion concerning many of their brave young men who had been through this awful conflict and that almost every day fresh information about this one or that one seeped through.

He then kindly suggested that Hannah might try visiting the offices of the British War Graves Commission situated just off the Elverdingestraat since, on occasion, they had information pertaining to German personnel, particularly if they had, at some point, been taken prisoner.

Hannah stepped out of the grey-brick building in Langemark and into the raw February air once more in order to retrace her steps and then to locate the next stop on her mission. As she traipsed her way back to the town centre, the sky grew angry and a fine, biting rain began to fall. It suited her mood perfectly.

And so she had arrived at the Commission with forlorn hope but in a last, desperate effort to find some sort of closure to the hole of despair she had been carrying in her heart for the past ten years.

# FINAL CURTAIN

Amy listened sympathetically to Hannah's story, just as she had listened to many other such stories during the past two and a half years. The fact that it had to do with a German soldier made no difference to her. With the benefit, or otherwise, of that sometimes pernicious measure called hindsight, the senseless bloodshed and the cost in human tragedy it brought in its wake on both sides of the trenches had become ever more obvious to all.

When Hannah had finished recounting her tale, Amy asked her to wait a moment while she went into the records room across the reception area to see if she could find any documentation that might throw some light upon Hannah's search.

There were just three large, slightly rusted, green filing cabinets marked quite simply 'GERMAN' in which any information pertaining to German military personnel that had come their way was carefully filed. Amy skimmed through the alphabetically listed folders to 'Z'.

Yes, there was just one 'Zimmermann'. But it was a Thomas, not a Jens; and listed as a 36 year old *Feldwebel*, a sergeant, which did not match the description that Hannah had given her. And besides, he had been attached to a different regiment.

With genuine sadness, Amy returned to the warm, little interview room and, as she had had to do on so many occasions to so many others, explained to Hannah as gently as she could that unfortunately the Commission did not hold any information concerning her son.

'Well, thank you for trying, Mrs Carpenter. I suppose it was a rather vain hope. But I had to check, you see. Just in case.'

'Yes. I understand. And I am sincerely sorry that we are not able to help you.

'What will you do now, if I may enquire?'

'I feel I have reached the end of the road and it has proven to be an impasse. I shall take the train tomorrow and return to Sigmaringen. You see, although, as I told you, I am originally from England, I feel Germany is very much my home. And as I mentioned, my dear husband is buried there.'

With that she stood up, offered her hand to Amy and thanked her once again for her time.

Then, as she reached the door, she hesitated slightly, turned and with a smile said, 'By the way, isn't it funny, Mr Carpenter, that you and I should share the same name?'

'Really?' answered Amy with a puzzled look.

'Oh, forgive me! Yes. You see, *Zimmermann* in English means 'carpenter'!' And with that she left.

Amy stood baffled for a moment. Then, with a casual shrug of her shoulders, returned to the records room to continue sorting new documents, which had been delivered the previous day and through which she had been wading, before the brief interlude with Frau Zimmermann.

As Hannah stepped back into the street and made her way solemnly towards the main square and thence to the guesthouse, the icy drizzle continued to weep from the heavy clouds overhead, bringing with it a feeling of leaden despair.

'Well,' she thought to herself, 'I have done my best. I've exhausted all avenues, my darling boy, but I cannot find you. Wherever you might be, may you rest in peace. Dear Jens…'

Then, momentarily reflecting on the translation of her surname for Mrs Carpenter, she recalled, 'And *Jens* in English would of course be 'Jack', wouldn't it?'

With that she pulled the collar of her coat more tightly

around her against the monotonous rain and headed for the guesthouse, to pack her things for the long journey back home. And back to loneliness.

# POSTSCRIPT

Hannah Zimmermann lived out the rest of her lonely day in the little town on the Danube. She visited Emil' grave twice a week and each evening she would sit by th window looking out onto the river as it rolled by on it ceaseless journey. She would look at the photograph of Jen and try to be thankful for the few years she had had with him

And then she would weep for the many years that she di not.

◊◊◊

As for Amy, she found love again.

On returning to England in 1931, she met and married th handsome curate who came to take on the parish when he father retired. They had two children.

Amy found happiness and fulfilment in meeting th demands both of motherhood and the rôle of a clergyman' wife.

She always kept the little silver locket engraved with a crocus given to her by the man whose memory still lingered in a secret corner of her heart.

◊◊◊

In another corner, that of a peaceful Flanders field, not far from the pretty town of Ypres, is a small military cemetery. It is one of dozens that lie scattered across the gentle countryside of that once war-ravaged land, with their neat, precise rows of bleach-white headstones, green grass and carefully tended borders.

At the far end of row H is one of those countless headstones inscribed with the simple words:

A SOLDIER OF THE GREAT WAR
KNOWN UNTO GOD

Each year, at the foot of that headstone, as winter melts into spring, a tiny golden crocus fights its way up through the brown earth into the day and blossoms like a small droplet of sunlight.

Printed in Great Britain
by Amazon